ORPHANS
Book 3 of the 'Toget

DEDICATION

Hi everyone

This is my third novella in the *Together Forever* series, and I hope you are enjoying the three young Guardians journey as much as I am, bringing them to life on the pages before you. It really is a joy continuing their adventures but it is even nicer to receive such glowing reviews, and for that I thank you all very much. I have big plans with how the series continues and there will be many more tales to tell before the Guardians hang up their staffs!

I certainly could never have got any of these books into your hands without the fantastic editing and proofreading of Dave Kingdon from Devon-proofreading. His great work, expert advice and valuable inspiration has helped produce all three novellas to the standard I was only hoping for. Thank you, Dave.

A lot of the places portrayed in Orphans in Time are based on real locations that are close to my heart. The Thurle Stone actually exists and is located off Thurlestone beach, Thurlestone, South Devon. Thurlestone holds a special place in my heart, it is my spiritual home. Many times, as a child, I would climb around the rock pools, cliffs and beaches, pretending I was in my own far flung adventure. Burgh island at Bigbury is where the Guardians come across the first nest of Dragons.

The Tor at Glastonbury is also a truly magical place, you can almost taste it. I always dreamt that it could be partly hollow with hidden treasures beneath, so to bring my dreams into the real world, (well, at least in these pages) was the proverbial dream come true.

Dartmoor is also alive with myths and legends. I walk there often with my two dogs, Cody and Peggy, often thinking up these stories as I wander from one Tor to the next, or through the forests that border the moor, feeling the age and mysticism that surrounds this wonderful part of our country.

With places like these firmly ensconced in my mind, inspiration comes quite easily, so I am truly blessed, living here over the years.

I dedicate this novella to all the people and friends who inspire me with their kind words of encouragement and advice, my long-suffering work colleagues, who I badger into reading the books, and of course all of you that have kindly purchased, read and reviewed them.

If you could kindly please leave feedback on Amazon and Goodreads, that would be much appreciated, thank you.

A quick plug, I am putting the three novellas together in one volume, *The Books of Time*, which will be released before Christmas 2020.

I hope you enjoy this chapter in Sam's, Chloe's and Jazz's education as young Guardians.

Best wishes

Ian P Marshall
November 11th 2020

CONTENTS

Chapter 1 - AND INTO THE FIRE
Chapter 2 - THE DEAD FOREST
Chapter 3 - MUTUALISM
Chapter 4 - THE THURLE STONE
Chapter 5 - DRAGONS END
Chapter 6 - AVALON
Chapter 7 - DESOLATION
Chapter 8 - RETURN TO AVALON
EPILOGUE

CHARACTERS, PLACES AND ARTEFACTS

Characters

Sam - Our inquisitive young adventurer and Guardian of the Earth
Jazz - The most authoritative of the three and Guardian of the Earth
Chloe - The third of the *Together forever* trio and Guardian of the Earth
Thorfell - A Pixie Prince assigned by Lancelot to help the Guardians
Lancelot - The missing Guardian and Knight of the Round Table
Guinevere - Lancelot's wife and Fairy Queen
Tristan Lorofax - Squire to Lancelot and future Knight
King Arthur - The King and Leader of the Round Table
Peggy - The baby Dragon!
George - A Knight of the Round Table
Cedric - The Gatekeeper and former warrior friend of Lancelot
The Anunaki - A race of beings from the dawn of time
Krall - A Skree warrior
Skree - A race of beings from the First Age of Man, who have been imprisoned beneath the Earth for centuries
DemonSkree - A larger breed of Skree who originate from Siberia, Russia
Erlking - A race of beings who control the Skree and rule the lower depths of the prison beneath the Earth
Moribund - Former Guardian of the Earth who turned evil
Shadowchasers - The Guardians' shadow warriors

Places

Avalon - The island of Avalon, the Capital and epicentre of the Kingdom, located at the end of the Bridge of Travel
The Thurle Stone - The Last remaining Hag stone in the future

Hag Stones - Magical stones that can transport you to different places and times with the correct calling
Tor Burr - The ancient name for Glastonbury Tor

Artefacts

The Books of Time - A magical and powerful book, showing the Three Ages of Mankind
Spear of Destiny - A spear of immense power forged in the distant past
Hall of Antiquities - A great hall on Avalon where powerful artefacts from across the world are kept safe
Bridge of Travel - A bridge that spans the fairy kingdom that leads to Avalon

CHAPTER 1 - AND INTO THE FIRE

"I need to tell you about the history of this world, before the Three Ages of Man, before the Books were created." Lancelot said, his face pensive. It had taken them most of the night to walk across the barren blackened landscape, scarred and burnt out trees, smouldering like smoking chimneys. A near full moon hidden behind the bank of low clouds, occasionally cast a monochromatic picture that made the three Guardians look on in horror at a countryside that was unrecognisable and alien in appearance. It wasn't until dawn broke that the complete horrifying picture was revealed. Giant working pits had been dug all over the ground, pock marking the land as if some god had reached down and wrenched out great handfuls of earth. Sam had seen pictures of the battlegrounds of the First World War, and to her, this was what it looked like the most, but on an even bigger scale. Walkways could be seen cut into the holes leading down to more, darker openings along the way. At times as they neared the pits, the air had an acrid smell and it became increasingly more difficult to breathe. Pools of water lay in some of these pits, the water looked dank and oily. Rainbow patterns swirled about the surface and the occasional ripple showed that some life remained within the depths. There was no sign of any Human habitation. No roads, no telegraph poles or communication masts. No buildings, nothing, it was as if Humans didn't exist. Sam had always wondered about the Earth if Humans were not upon it. In her mind, she pictured it as a beautiful place, where wildlife held sway and the land was a forest of meadows and woodlands, with herds of different animals living in harmony and tranquility. What Sam saw now was the polar opposite of this picture. Lancelot led them as well as he could through this, moving from cover to cover, his steps assured and

steady, waving them on in silence with an urgency that made Sam feel nervous, as if they were being hunted. At one stage, a Dragon swooped out of the clouds to dive down and glide over their hiding spot. Hidden in a small cairn of stones, Lancelot and Guinevere, pulled them tight and told them to close their eyes. Sam remembered hearing the swoosh of the wings and felt the great beast pass close overhead, and disappear again into the clouds, before she let out a deep breath and opened her eyes. They waited there for what felt like an eternity before Guinevere nodded to Lancelot and they set off again at a brisk pace. They were heading gradually downhill and as the sun rose, they glimpsed the sea before them in the distance. At another time a contingent of Skree were leading a group of near naked, bedraggled Humans to they knew not where. Chained together, the group of twenty Humans moved as one beneath the watchful eyes of their captors, their bearded faces kept low in abeyance, their bodies ravaged and thin. An Erlking led the troop, marching in front as if he were someone of great importance, seemingly oblivious to the group he led. A low murmuring came from the Humans that made Sam want to cover her head and scream. Apart from this, the land was silent and deserted, not a bird sang, not an insect moved, it was as if all life had vanished from the Earth. In places a low mist, almost like steam, drifted up out of the ground as if the Earth itself was breathing.

As the sun rose, so Lancelot forced the pace. The sea loomed ever nearer and as they reached an area where gorse held sway atop a headland, he stopped. Peering behind him one final time, he pulled some broken gorse away to reveal a hidden path behind. They all entered and Lancelot quickly replaced the gorse. He peered up praying that he would not see movement above and saw no sign apart from the billowing low cloud and sultry atmosphere. Sam noticed that Guinevere was choking badly, and Lancelot raced to her side to offer support. Arm in arm they led the three Guardians through a labyrinth of gorse to the top of a cliff, and then without pausing seemed to step right off the edge. When Sam reached the cliff edge, she noticed a small line of protruding stone steps, that formed a narrow path, leading down the cliff face to a small opening. Thorfell let out a short, shrill whistle before gripping tight to her lapel. He hadn't said a word since returning, his thoughts his own. Gulping deeply, she followed Lancelot and Guinevere with Jazz and Chloe close behind. Waves crashed on the rocks a long way below her, the noise refreshingly loud and normal. She took a deep breath in, the air tasting salty but clearer, more as it should taste and smell. With their backs to the rock face they shuffled down, until eventually they reached the opening and were beckoned in rapidly by Lancelot, who continued to look out for any sign of being seen. Shepherding them in, he then pulled more gorse across to cover the opening. They entered and stood in a low ante-chamber in the cave, the partial light from outside showing that apart from some bushes that had been hastily cut and used as camouflage, the place was bare. An opening in the cave showed light beyond, and following Lancelot between a narrow gap in the rock, they entered into another ante-chamber, this one lit by a torch. To the left of the circular cavern, a stream of water passed through, its age-old passage denoted by the depression in the stone that had been worn down over countless centuries. A small fire was burning, its embers in need of more fuel. Above their heads they could see the odd root poking through the ceiling, the roots somehow forcing their way through the tiniest of cracks in the stone. Some armour and a small amount of provisions leant against the back wall. A spear that had tarnished gold bands around it, and an iron point with some sort of jewel at its tip, stood upright against the wall, the light from the fire making the gold shine. Some sort of rug or cloth was placed alongside one wall. Guinevere sat beside the fire, her face ashen and tight lipped. The face was now lined and aged, her once beautiful complexion, pale and haggard. Her features flickered in the fire light, giving her an almost ghostly translucent look. Her beautiful light green eyes now seemed tarnished and dark. Even her blonde hair seemed dull, lifeless and streaked with grey. Sam noticed that she was shaking and swaying as if to keep warm. Lancelot wrapped a blanket around her shoulders and this she held tight around her frame, holding onto it with both hands. She looked up at them and forced a smile. Only a few days previous, she had looked so young and alive, now she looked as if she was dying.

Lancelot turned to the girls and spoke at last. Even he had aged. His shoulders were slumped, his back, normally so straight and regal was arched, giving him the bent over look of an old man. His face was lined and his once flowing black hair was also now mottled with streaks of grey. After the revelation that they had failed, he hadn't spoken since.

"Welcome to our humble abode," he said with no hint of humour, stretching his hands wide to encompass the cave. His voice, at least, sounded the same.

"What's happened?" Jazz asked.

"What is going on?" Chloe continued. "And what do you mean, 'we lost'?"

"I think you had better come and sit down," Guinevere said coughing, and placing her hand on the floor to ask them to join her. "We've got some pretty bad news you need to hear before we talk about anything else!"

Sam was still shocked, her mind was racing, trying to keep up. Words would not form in her mind let alone on her lips so she walked with the others towards Guinevere, and sat down. Lancelot gathered some firewood and started to rekindle the fire, it's crackling and burning loud in the confines of the cave. The smoke drifted high into the darkness and dispersed out of a small hole high up.

"You need to know before I tell you," Guinevere started, "that this can all be undone. As Moribund has changed this, then so too can we," she paused breathing in, and they could all see the effort she was taking just to speak. "Everything is gone. Your homes, your family and friends, civilisation that you know of, never happened."

The three girls, sat wide eyed. Sam put her hand to her mouth to stifle a cry as tears ran freely down her cheeks. She felt her body trembling in fear of what Guinevere had said. Jazz put her head in her hands and started to sob. Chloe was shaking uncontrollably, nodding her head as if to shake out the lie in the truth. Sam felt numb! Thorfell whimpered on her shoulder and leant into her. She could hear his tiny cries as he tried to come to terms with things, but her mind was in so much turmoil, she had no reply to give him. Her mum, her dad, gone, never existed; no McDonald's, TV, her cats, her home, school, civilisation! Her thoughts and her world were in absolute turmoil. She swayed and reached out, feeling the cold hard stone beneath her fingers as she tried to stay sitting upright. She tried to calm her breathing, she felt the fast beating of her heart and thought she was having some sort of panic attack. 'Breathe, Sam,' she said to herself, 'breathe,' As her pulse began to slow, so she suddenly became aware that she could sense her mind moving down through the cold rock and out into the ocean. In her mind, she could hear the movements of the sea and all of its denizens. She sensed the millions of creatures that inhabited the depths from the smallest of barnacles right through to largest of whales. At least here within the sea and the mass of the oceans, life seemed to be normal. It was just then, as she was thinking this, that a shadow passed across her senses, a coldness that was different to anything else, it gave her chill as if she had been touched by death itself. She felt the creatures around her in the ocean react the same and swim away from it. Something huge and evil lurked in the depths, something that was alien to the water and should not be there, something that now sensed her. An eye opened in the darkness of this shadow, searching for her ... She lifted her hand off the stone, a cold sweat forming across her body. 'What was that?' Her reverie was broken.

"How ..." Chloe said through sobs, "How are we here, if our parents didn't exist?"

"You are from a different time, my dear. That timeline still exists ... and will do again, one day, if we can change things back to where they were. Do not despair, Guardians, all is not lost," she said, reaching out, putting her arms around all three, as they huddled together waiting for the girls to gather themselves.

"What has happened to you?" Jazz asked. "How did you get here?"

"I will answer that. Rest, my love," Lancelot said to Guinevere, "you need to conserve your energy. And it is time to release some more," he said to her. They both rose then, Lancelot helping Guinevere up. They approached the stream and at the same time, placed one hand in the water for what seemed like about ten seconds. Guinevere's eyes were shut while Lancelot stared into the darkness of the cave, his bright eyes, gleaming and seeming to pulse in the darkness, his thoughts dark and troubled.

They returned to the fire and sat down and Lancelot replied to a couple of raised eyebrows and questioning looks. "They track us by the magic that is within us," he said, "if we don't disperse some into the water, it builds up and they will find us. That is why here is the best place for us to be, beside the sea, where the magic will be gone as soon as it reaches the water. But they will find us eventually, we know that," he said smiling sadly at Guinevere. "We are the only ones left. They search for us day and night, never stopping. They are relentless. It is only a matter of time, that is why time is of the essence for you to return, before all is lost. You see, mes amis, we are dying. We have only been here two days. The magic that keeps us, especially Guinevere, alive, the Earth magic, is nearly gone. It is so weak in this timeline, that when that disappears ..." he left the sentence unfinished. "It is that same magic that they track us by. Guardians, please do not summon your shadowchasers unless it is the only option. In this reality, any magic you use is like a beacon to the Dragons."

"Like a homing beacon, a *find my phone* satellite image," Chloe said matter-of-factly.

"Something like that," he replied with a faint smile.

Sam's mind suddenly shot back to moments before, when she felt the magic coursing out of her and into the ocean. 'Had the Dragons picked that up,' she thought, her mind panicking.

"How did you get here? How did you know that we would come through that stone?" Jazz asked, breaking Sam's worrying thoughts.

"Because the ones in our realm are gone, that realm was never formed by the Books of Time after the first great battle. There was no first great battle or we did not win it, I do not know. It seems Moribund went back in time and rewrote history to his liking. From what we have learned, Humans are born and bred into captivity. Erlking and Skree run the mines, forcing the Humans to work until they drop, while Dragons fill the sky. For centuries now, this has been going on. All of the history that you know of, never happened."

"That is the last stone that Thorfell knows the incantation for. If you were going to appear at all, it could only be there," he turned and nodded to Thorfell. "Good job, my friend, you have done well, none of this is your fault. We came through the same stone, two days hence. We were in the magic realm, sitting on some rocks, looking out over the moor, when it hit us. It was like being visibly struck, but it was a mental wave, so powerful it knocked us to the floor. When we rose, to our horror, we could see the land being consumed, eaten up into nothingness like a giant tsunami of antilife. Behind it was nothing and it was racing towards us from every angle as if we were the focal point of this assault. We raced back to the cavern, running down the stairs two at a time, even as the stones above us started to be drawn into this vortex of nothingness. I grabbed some weapons, reached for the Book, but only came away with a blank page as that too was drawn away from us, sucked into the vacuum. We headed through the Hag stone, towards your realm thinking we would be safe there, but we came out here," he said, looking towards Guinevere whose head was lowered in silent contemplation. "We left everyone else there to die, we could not save them, we knew that. Finding you was what we had to do. We had to find out what happened. Why history has changed and how to change it back?"

"The magic realm is gone?" Thorfell said slowly, realising now that he was truly alone. His legs buckled and he slid down Sam's jacket to land on her outstretched palm. He hopped off it and walked out the narrow opening, his head low. Sam started to rise to go after him but a hand on her shoulder stopped her.

"Let him go, he needs solitude now, he will be OK," Lancelot said looking into her eyes.

"Please tell us everything that happened to you and do not leave anything out, we must find out how this has happened and do not worry, I know what you are thinking, because this is the only time line, the laws of having to leave within the day do not apply here. Do not fear, we can still get home," he paused, "we will get home," he added.

After explaining what had transpired and answering as many questions as they could remember the answers to, Lancelot sat in silence, his eyes staring into the fire as if it were some crystal ball that would give him the answers he needed. Guinevere hadn't moved, her thoughts her own.

"I remember that day well, the day that Arthur was poisoned. I remember you now. I remember throwing a spear through Moribund, knowing that it wouldn't kill him, he is still a Guardian, so he cannot be killed by a mere spear. Since our entrance into this world, Moribund has been destroying all the Hag stones so that we cannot go back in time and change history, like he has done. If he succeeds, then we will be trapped here for all time. If the Dragons destroy the Hag Stone upon the moor, that you came through, then there is only one stone I know of that is left. But they don't know about it because only we know of it, even Sol and Percival didn't know of it. And its been in plain sight for centuries. The only problem is it's further down the coast and worse still, it's in the sea!" he said with one of his boyish grins.

"What," said Jazz, "in the sea?"

"And it's further down the coast, you say?" Sam asked, her mind starting to put things together. "And it's in the sea?" she asked again, and before Lancelot could reply, she added. "You mean Thurlestone Rock, don't you, the rock with the big hole in, that's in the sea?"

"Got it in one, ma cherie, very astute, young Guardian," he said nodding in admiration.

"That's a Hag stone? In the sea."

"At low tide, it is easy to get to. At high tide, it is submerged. If you come back through at the wrong time, you might come through into the sea!"

"Great, we're going to get wet," Jazz said, eyes wide.

"Or drown!" added Chloe.

"That sounds more like the Jazz we know," Sam said, chuckling to herself.

"Thurle is a derivative of old English for hole, Thirl, which then became, Thurle Stone, Thurlestone, except it's not called that in this timeline." Guinevere added.

"I need to tell you about the history of this world, before the Three Ages of Man, before the Books were created." Lancelot said, his face pensive. "This way you will understand the history of the world and what we need to do to put things right. You see, before the First Age, there was another time. No one quite knows exactly how it all started. Some say a great craft arrived, and with it the owners of this craft brought with it different races as slaves. They built huge empires and ruled over the Earth with a rod of iron. Humans, Lizardmen, Giants and others were all slaves to these creatures, that some now call the Anunaki. They manipulated the genes of these creatures experimenting with their DNA. Eventually some cataclysm happened that forced these Anunaki to leave quickly. They took as many slaves as they could with them, but left just as many behind. Some survived this cataclysm, the Lizardmen heading south to the warmer climes, while the Humans were driven north into the colder more mountainous regions. Of the Giants, little is known other than that only a few survived and lived their lives out in secrecy in the deep jungles of Kush. Occasional stories of two headed Giants arose over the centuries, but that is all. Folktales, myths and legends are steeped with Giants and their like. And, of course, we have our own Giants in Cornwall. After many years the Humans decided to migrate south towards the sun and the rich green valleys that would more easily sustain them. A delegation was sent to the Lizardmen asking to live in harmony with them. They did not return. The Lizardmen obviously were not too keen on this and the first ever war broke out. After centuries of fighting the Humans drove them out and took control of the Earth. Hyperborea was created, dawning an age of wonder and enlightenment. Shining cities and Kingdoms were spawned. Atlan-

tis was at its centre. Wars were fought, empires won and lost. In the background the remaining Lizardmen had evolved taking on Human guise and living among the Humans, planning and plotting to overthrow them. Eventually a great King of Atlantis found out their plans and vowed to wipe them from the Earth. By his side was a fearsome warrior whose magical spear never missed its mark. Together they hunted down the Lizardmen until they were nearly extinct. Forging great weapons, an axe and shield which the King used, they very nearly succeeded too, but some escaped. Then, a second great cataclysm happened, the seas rose and wiped out this Age from the face of the Earth. Only the odd archeological find hints back to that grand era, so widespread was the destruction. But again, Human and Lizard survived until the First Age of Man dawned. It was upon the moor that the next great battle was fought and won by us. It was there that we forged the Books of Time and imprisoned the Lizardmen beneath the earth."
There was a stunned silence when Lancelot stopped.
"So, we were put here by aliens?" Chloe asked.
"Well, if you put it that way ... yes," Lancelot replied with a frown.
"Cool," she replied with a lopsided smile.
"How do you know these things?" Jazz asked.
"Stories, legends passed down over the centuries, tales of old. Am I not a legend in your time, Guinevere too?" he asked rhetorically with a twinkle in his eye. "And we have artefacts, proof, you've seen the Skree, you know they are real. What we are asking you to do is retrieve one of these artefacts for me ..." he paused.
"You mean steal it?" Sam asked.
"We will put it back once it has served its purpose," replied Lancelot.
"Which is?" Jazz enquired.
"To kill Moribund, to end this, once and for all. We know where he is going to be, we know I will hit him with a spear at Tor Burr. If I hit him with the right spear, we can stop all this madness from happening," he said sweeping his arms wide to encompass the world that they were now in. "Are you up for taking another trip, back to the same place, to make things right?"

"Of course," Sam heard herself saying. "We will do anything it takes to make this right."
"Definitely," Chloe added with a wink towards Sam.
"Yes," Jazz replied, eyebrows raised, "we are Guardians, after all. What do you need us to do?"
"You need to go back to the same day again, head into the tunnel, not up the steps. Go to the Abbey and find my Squire, he's called Tristan, he will be a great knight one day, but at the moment, he's just a young apprentice. Explain you need to get to Avalon and retrieve the ancient spear of Lemuria. Tell him to leave it at the back of the cavern hidden out of sight, beside the entrance to the well. If he doesn't believe you, show him your rings and tell him that *time is a law that has no respect for who you are*. He once said that to me. He is fixated on time, always has been."
"Won't we bump into ourselves and cause some sort of time thing, like we will just cease to exist or something?" Jazz asked.
"You will enter the place a few minutes before or after. I have done this once before with Sol and Percival. Somehow, you come out at a slightly different moment each time. It's as if time itself knows and throws you in at a different time, each jump."
"OK, that sounds a bit weird!" Chloe said, looking pensively towards the other two.
"We'll do it," Jazz said, "whatever it takes."
"OK, thank you, mes amis. If all goes well, the journey will take you a day to get to Thurl stone Rock. You must use your wits and cunning to evade the Skree hunting gangs, and the Dragons. They will be drawn to your magic like a moth to a light. Follow the sea and if you need to head inland at any time, stay close to water. I don't know what you will find out there but you must be prepared for anything ... anything! You have your staffs, your shadowchasers cannot be summoned, or the Dragons would be upon you straight away. Only as a last resort will you use your shadowchasers, promise me?"
"Of course, we understand, don't we ladies ... Guardians," Chloe said correcting herself.

◆ ◆ ◆

Sam rose quietly and slipped through the narrow opening and into the outer cavern. She stopped to take in her surroundings, waiting for her eyes to become accustomed to the darkness in this cavern. Through the concealed entrance a faint light shone through from outside and a warm breeze ruffled her dirty hair. She pushed her way through and stood on the ledge looking out over the ocean, illuminated by a full moon that hung heavy within a scattering of clouds. She heard the sea first, the rhythmic crashing of the waves against the rocks. The mists had lifted for now, giving the sea a look of dark shadows and white tipped sea horses that shone in the moon's dull light and were gone again in a heartbeat. She peered back up the way they had entered and there was no sign of the steps that they had taken to reach here. 'Not all magic has gone, not yet, anyway,' she thought, shaking her head.
She gazed out into the vastness of the ocean, her thoughts sombre and worried. Her heart hung heavy she felt the weight of the world on her shoulders. Without any fear, she sat down on the floor near the edge and crossed her legs, pulling them up tight.
"Mind if I join you?" Jazz said quietly.
"Be my guest," she replied.
"You OK?" Jazz asked sitting down next to her.
For a few moments, Sam didn't reply. "We are not even fifteen years old and we have the task of saving the world, it seems ridiculous, it's like one of the films or series that Chloe would watch, but this is the real thing. We have no family, no friends, everything is gone, yet that bit doesn't seem to bother me, yet it almost seems unreal, as if it's not true. So, no, I'm not OK with that, but I'm OK apart from that."
"We are not just teenagers anymore, we are Guardians now," Jazz said.
"Yes, I know, but we are teenagers first and we have had only one day's training, I don't think that qualifies us a fully fledged members of the Guardians clan."

"Lancelot said we were born to be Guardians, I believe him, so it was always meant to be us that faces this quest."
"Are you saying we were destined to be the ones? That we had no say in the matter? You know we have never really talked about anything since it started, it's been such a rollercoaster ride, that none of us have really just sat down and spoken about our fears, we've just got on with it."
Jazz stared out to sea, for a change, lost for a reply, momentarily.
"No, we haven't, but we can when this is all over, I promise. In McDonald's at Marsh Mills," she said with a smile.
Sam smiled back, nodding. "Deal." she replied. "But I prefer KFC!"
They both laughed at the thought and immediately looked behind them to make sure they hadn't been heard. Sam looked at her hands clasped together in her lap, and spoke a little more quietly.
"You know, it's down to us now, us alone. Lancelot and Guinevere are ageing by the hour, they can't come with us, they would give our position away anyway. I don't know how long they have left, but it's down to us now," she repeated, "the three of us, to put this right!"
'Make that four," a high-pitched voice said from behind a rock. Thorfell, she'd forgotten about him. "I need to help bring our realm back," he said solemnly, walking around the rock to sit down beside them. "My friends and family too."
"You know, the worst thing is that if we succeed, and we will, I promise," said Jazz, "is that we will remember everything, this place, this evil realm, it will always be with us for all time."
"Then let's make it the motivation to stop this realm from happening," Chloe said from behind them, walking towards them and sitting down. "I can't sleep either," she added with a wink.
Sam stared at Chloe for a second, smiled, and then returned her gaze towards the sea.
"We are going to get home," Jazz said again, sensing Sam's dark mood.
"Do you think we ever existed in this timeline?" Chloe asked.
"You never know, we might be out there somewhere in some

form, but I doubt it. Somehow, I feel we are orphans in this world, this timeline," Sam said thoughtfully.

"Orphans in time," Chloe replied solemnly.

"Exactly," Sam replied.

CHAPTER 2 - THE DEAD FOREST

They left at dawn disappearing into the gorse, to the right of where Lancelot had entered the night before. A sea mist dulled their senses making the sea sound muffled and brought visibility down to only a few paces in front of them.
"Follow the coast, stay as close as you can to the sea, until you see the rock," Lancelot had told them. 'Well, 'thought Sam, 'I can't even see my hand in front of my face at the moment!' Never had she felt so vulnerable in her life. They could walk into a Skree hunting party at any moment, so bad was the visibility. They could even walk off the end of the cliff if they were not alert. The gorse quickly disappeared to be replaced by a sea of giant ferns, some almost as high as them. They passed through these with an ease that they thought would not be possible on first sight. The ground beneath their feet was soft and green and almost *normal*. They eventually, and very suddenly, stepped out of the ferns to see that swathes and swathes had been burnt to the ground making the going relatively easy, but in a much more dangerous way. As the sun rose, so they looked ahead for shelter and at times there was none. The land itself looked foreboding and dead, almost as if the Earth itself had given up living. At times there were few trees, even burnt ones, so they had to race across open ground to reach the next cover of ferns or burnt tree stumps. Crossing open spaces was one of the scariest things Sam had ever done. She felt the eyes of the world were watching her and she was waiting for a scream to go up, and then a chase would ensue. Twice already, they had seen in the distance, groups of Skree and an Erlking leading shackled humans towards an unknown destination. They had concealed themselves and waited while Thorfell watched them move away and out of sight. Those times had been long moments of silent contemplation and the fear of being found out. If they got captured, she dreaded what would happen

to them. She tried not to think of that! They stayed as close to the cliffs as they could, making their way through the burnt landscape at a slow but steady pace. No landmark was visible, the land rolled up and down in front them like a wave. Even though the sun was up, the sky was still covered in low cloud and the smell of Sulphur lingered in their senses, making them choke at times. Covering their mouths, they would cough as quietly as they could and then move on, never stopping. Despite the misty drizzle from earlier, the day was now warm and their clothes stuck to them, uncomfortably. Thorfell sat on Sam's shoulder, holding on to her lapel and issuing instructions as best he could. His vision seemed to be almost heightened by their tricky situation and when they stopped briefly for a snack, under a burnt tree, he explained that all Pixies had fantastic vision and could even see in the dark.

"Now you tell us!" Chloe said.

They sat huddled together in the shadows, while Thorfell sat atop a charcoaled branch watching for any sign of pursuit. Rocks littered the landscape at this point and this was like a double-edged sword. In one hand it was great cover, in the other it was also great cover for the things that might be looking out for them. A tightness wrapped around Sam as if she was being suffocated in cling film. She almost felt she couldn't breathe properly. They approached a fast-flowing stream, about ten feet wide and a few feet deep, that smelt like a cesspit and looked even worse. A fallen tree covered the crossing and they clambered up and over, to the other side, with much relief. Once across, Sam reached down and was about to touch the water when Thorfell stopped her with a shrill shout of warning. "Not this one, this one is bad, we will find another soon," he warned her. She looked down at her oily reflection and hardly recognised the girl that looked back. Something beneath the surface, something quite large, broke her reflection into a hundred tiny ripples and she stood up with a start and stepped back quickly.

As they clambered through rocks to the top of another rise, an unusual sight beheld them. They all stood up in amazement, looking down on a forest that stretched before them from the sea to their right, as far as they could see inland and as far as they could see in front of them. But this was no ordinary forest. It seemed to consist mainly of fir but not a fir like they had ever seen before. The needles that hung from the trees looked a sickly washed out brown colour. The whole forest looked dead. If it were a painting it almost seemed as if the colour had been taken out of it, like it had been drained of all life. Some trees stood tall and erect, but somehow looked lost amongst the rest. A lot of trees had collapsed to lay against each other, half fallen but propped up by its neighbours. Some had not been so lucky and lay upon the floor, their roots exposed to the air, looking like toppled statues. They could see burn marks upon some of the trees and Sam wondered how the whole forest had not been burnt to the ground. The forest gave off a feeling of decay and darkness that hung heavy beneath its canopy. A faint buzzing could be heard coming from within and the girls all looked each other, eyes wide. The forest creaked like an old house, the light wind making the tops of the trees sway this way and that. Within the overhang, shadows hung heavy and with the slight movement of the trees in the wind so it almost seemed as if there was movement from within. From where they stood, a piece of open ground swept down before them to the forest, and to Sam this looked as if it was a barrier between the forest on one side and the land on the other.

"Creepy!" Chloe said in a spooky voice.

"We could go around it, by the beach?" Jazz said, pointing to the coast.

No one fancied entering the forest, no words needed to be spoken, the whole place gave off a haunted feeling, and Sam again felt as if she was been watched. Anyone could be hiding within the line of the trees looking at them right now!

"Good plan," Sam said, as Thorfell started tugging on her ear.

A shrill screech went up behind them, making their blood turn to ice. 'We have been spotted!' Sam thought, as panic gripped her like coming out of a bad dream.

"Thirteen Skree, a mile back coming this way fast!" Thorfell stated with a tiny gulp.

"Unlucky for some," Chloe replied dryly.

"We have to move, ladies!" Jazz said, eyes wide, staring behind her as another shriek went up. Like a basket of snakes spilled to the ground so the Skree spread out and came towards them at pace, eating up the ground quicker than they had ever seen them move before.

"Let's go," Sam said, "Thorfell, hold on tight, we are going into the forest, it's our only chance of getting away."

Without another word they set off, racing down the hill as fast as their legs could carry them. They raced through the rocks, slipping and sliding part of the way down, before levelling off onto the bare ground. The forest came ever closer, the trees larger now than they had thought at first. A tiny opening could be seen in the trees, as if it were an animal run but no animals were alive, as far as they knew. High up in the branches, they spotted circular holes a few feet wide and at regular intervals as if someone had drilled into the forest. The first Skree appeared on top of the rise, when the Guardians were about halfway to the cover of the trees, and let out another shrill cry before bounding on down the hill towards them. 'We aren't going to make it!' Sam thought as she ran as fast as she could, while at the same time glancing over her shoulder to see the rest of the Skree top the rise and start down, like a tsunami of scales and talons. She tripped, stumbled and nearly fell before righting herself, fear gripping her muscles, her arms cartwheeling for balance. Chloe was ahead of her and also glancing back. Jazz was level with her. She looked in front towards the trees, they were still so far away. The shadows of the forest lay before them barely a hundred paces in front, when the first Skree reached them. Chloe stopped, turned and swung her staff in an arc as Sam and Jazz ducked and passed her. The Skree went down in a tangle of legs and arms, rolling to a halt in a ball of dusty earth.

"Keep going," Chloe shouted rejoining them as the Skree rose groggily, limping slightly and continuing after them. The rest of its brethren raced past it without a backwards glance closing in on the three young Guardians.

The girls crossed into the shadow of the forest and immediately felt a drop in temperature. A wail went up from the Skree behind them and Sam, breathing hard, looked over her shoulder to see that the Skree had all stopped just shy of the shadow line of the forest. Sam ground to a halt, glad to be stopping, her heart pounding, her lungs thankful for the respite.
"Stop, stop, Jazz, Chloe ... look!" Sam said as the other two ground to a halt and turned, staffs at the ready. A frown rose on both their faces as they looked at the Skree. They were screaming and shouting at them in some unintelligible language. From their body language they seemed to be berating the fact they hadn't caught them, but there was also something else about their actions, almost as if they knew that the Guardians weren't going to get away anyway. They seemed to be jeering at them. These Skree looked different to any they had ever seen, they seemed more comfortable standing upright, their legs were long and powerful, their backs straight, almost Human like. And then Sam realised that these Skree hadn't been living under the ground for centuries, they owned the world now, so they lived on the land not under it. That was the evolutionary difference of time, living without the confines beneath the ground.
"You know," said Chloe, peering at the Skree then over her shoulder at the forest. "This doesn't bode well!" she said. "In every film or show I've seen where the bad guys are stopped by fear of going any further and the good guys are relieved to have escaped their evil clutches, when they enter the place that the bad guys shun away from, it normally gets worse for the good guys!"
"Great! So, it's out of the frying pan and into the fire is it?" Jazz asked.
"Thats normally how it pans out." Chloe replied. "No pun intended!"
"Great," Sam added, "you're a bringer of good tidings!"
"Just stating the facts. Look they are leaving." Chloe said pointing. The Skree had turned their backs on the group and were heading back up the hill towards the rise, their chase over.
"They know we are here," Jazz said quietly, "they know about us

now, it won't be long before a Dragon or two come looking. We have to go through the trees, they will give us good cover. We must stay close to the coast though and keep a lookout for Thurl stone Rock. Wouldn't be good to miss it. We can't be that far away now."

"I agree with Jazz, makes perfect sense, but what I want to know is, what were those Skree so scared of to stop them coming any closer?"

As one, they turned and looked into the impenetrable darkness of the forest.

They entered under the overhang of the trees and headed along it until they reached a long sandy beach. The air felt still and the sound of the sea seemed muffled under the cover of the trees. The forest was so thick, that it seemed that only a few yards in, darkness held sway. Without the normal sounds of wildlife, the wood looked soulless and somehow incomplete, as if waiting for the coming of nature and man. The faint buzzing continued to be heard and it sounded to Sam like it came from deeper within the forest. Within a few minutes of following the tree line, Sam felt and sensed that she was being watched. Every pore in her body screamed at her that something was in there watching her. She remembered a lesson week from her Primary school, in Corntown, where they had gone through the five senses. Could there be another one, hidden or wiped clean by the evolution of Humanity. Most wild animals had it, they sensed fear when it was not visible to the eye and this is what she felt now. Something was in there, watching them, she knew that, she sensed it. Perhaps it was a new found power of being a Guardian that had awakened this sense. Her knuckles were white from gripping her staff so tight that her forearm and elbow were aching. 'Breathe, Sam,' she said to herself. As they neared the beach, they stopped and checked for any pursuit.

"They are gone," Thorfell said, reading their minds, and then added, "for now."

A wind had risen and the sea had turned rough, white horses littered the bay, and a fine mist hung in the air from the waves that crashed against the beach, racing up the slope towards them, before ebbing back down the smooth sand to rejoin the sea. The sea looked as if it were above them, the horizon seemed almost too high. Sam looked at the sand and momentarily smiled at the unblemished state of the beach, the smoothness of the sand and the thought that they were the first Humans to ever make footprints. There was not one single ...

"Footprint!" Chloe said stopping dead in her tracks. "Human!" she said pointing in front of her to a spot just out from the edge of the forest.

As one, they looked at the footprint, then toward the forest. Nothing moved. No sound could be heard over the roar of the waves. They approached the footprint and saw more heading out along the sand in the direction they were going before they headed back onto the harder ground towards the tree line. The footprints in the sand looked Human, but too small for an adult.

"A child," Jazz exclaimed.

"A young one too," Chloe added.

"Could it have escaped and now lives in the forest?" Thorfell asked.

"I suppose so," Sam replied, still sensing that she was being watched.

"Let's move on," Jazz said, "we need to keep going."

With a nod of approval and one final glance at the footprints, they carried on skirting the treeline as best they could. The tide was coming in fast and getting close to the trees in places. Sam could see the tideline barely a few feet from the trees. They turned a corner and Chloe, who was leading, tensed and threw herself to the sand, calling for all of them to get down behind a low line of jagged rocks that jutted out from a gradual rise to their left and disappeared into the ocean. An island loomed up before them shrouded in mist and what looked like smoke. High cliffs rose from the sea on three sides, while the landward facing side sloped down to join the beach. From their vantage point, they could see movement from on top of the small island. Some sort of structure sat atop the cliffs, but nothing made by man. It was more nestlike and huge in size. Chloe turned to them and silently pointed to the cliff's edge on the side facing them.

"Dragon!" she said wide-eyed in fear. Silhouetted against the sun, the huge form of a Dragon could be seen perched on the cliff edge, unmoving, seemingly asleep. One giant paw hung over the cliff edge, its long snout resting upon it, facing in their direction. 'Had they been seen? ' Sam wondered in panic. The creature lay stationary, the faint swish of the tip of its tail denoting the only sign of life.

"Dragons!" Thorfell squeaked from beside Sam's left ear as he pointed to the landward facing side. A Dragon appeared out of the shadows of the overhang of the cliffs, walking on thick powerful squat legs straight towards their hiding place. The Dragon was a good distance away but already Sam was looking for a better hiding place when movement on the other side of the rocks snapped her attention back to the present. A small head appeared above the rocks, all scales and teeth.

"Baby Dragon!" Jazz exclaimed in disbelief, as the creature, seeing the three girls and Thorfell, let out a loud shrill cry of alarm.

"Into the trees, now," she said as out of the corner of her eye, she saw the adult Dragon quicken its pace towards them. Huddling low, they clambered up a small incline and darted into a small gap in the trees, and kept going until they heard the sound of the dragon stop beside its young infant. Hiding behind some trees, they peered back through towards the beach. The Dragon hadn't seen them, but after looking down at the baby, which was trying to climb the rocks, it stood there a while, sniffing the air and peering into the trees. Its huge bulk blocked out the light and its footsteps, despite being muffled by the sand, still seemed to shake the earth. After a few more moments, it reached down and picked its baby up in its mouth and with a kick of its hind legs and push of its wings it swept up and away from them, leaving a trail of sand in its wake.

Sam let out a huge sigh. "That was close," she said quietly as if they might be overheard.
"Too close!" Jazz said.
"What do you mean?" Chloe asked.
"Didn't you see what was behind the island in the next bay on? It was the Thurl stone Rock, I'm sure of it. I saw it. So how are we supposed to get to that without being spotted by Dragon heart and his family?" she asked.
Sam raised her eyebrows. "We have to find a way otherwise we are trapped here forever!"
They all realised the consequences of this, so no reply was necessary. Looking about them, the trees looked grey to the eyes and diseased. Bark hung off the trunks in places as if the trees were shedding skin like a snake. The floor was littered with pine needles and rotting leaves, making the ground soft and spongy to walk on. Strange looking brambles with sharp barbs cluttered together in places, seemingly suffocating the trees in their lethal embrace. A faint sickly smell lingered in the air, making them pinch their noses in disgust.
They made their way through the trees, keeping the sea on their right and staying far enough in to keep out of sight of the Dragons. It was only a few minutes later when they glimpsed the end of the trees ahead of them, that they realised they had come to a large river mouth. The island was still visible to their right through the trees. They could see the two adult Dragons perched upon the top while the young one seemed to be practicing flying by launching itself off the top of the cliffs to swoop down, swing around and land in an ungraceful heap on the sand, only to clamber back up and do it again.
They quietly crept to the edge of the tree line and peered out. A wide river meandered its way to the sea through the forest, looking upriver, its course gradually disappeared into the trees. The river joined the sea in a wide inlet that opened out towards the island. The forest on the other side looked identical to the one on their side and seemed from their vantage point to go on forever.
"How are we going to cross that?" Sam asked.

"I can show you," said a young voice from behind them.

CHAPTER 3 - MUTUALISM

A young boy stood behind them, barely ten feet away. He was in his mid-teens, very thin and naked from the waist up. Dirt covered his youthful dishevelled face, and it reminded Sam of one of the chimney-sweeps from Mary Poppins. His ribs showed through his skin, like some evil skeleton that wished to push through and break free of the flesh that encompassed it. He gave them a quick smile with a raise of his cheeks, then relaxed and looked at them with a sense of wonder, mixed with fear.

"Come," he said, ushering them to follow, and Sam's eye's widened when she noticed that his lips were not moving, he was talking to them telepathically. Her mind drifted back to the Council of Elders and how they had conversed telepathically. Had this child somehow rekindled a new sense, just as the creatures from the Fairy Realm had been able to do?'

Sensing no malice, the three looked at each other, nodded and started following the boy through the woods.

"I don't think this is a good ..."

'It's OK, Thorfell, we've got this," Chloe said confidently. "And besides, we need to find a way to get across that river without becoming Dragon toast, and I think this boy might know how?"

A narrow path led through the trees and they followed this for some time. The noise of the river could be heard off to their right, through the trees. The young boy kept up a quick pace, with a confident swagger of one who knows where he is going. Occasionally, he would look behind him to check the girls were following, before racing forward, bobbing in and out of the trees in front of them, as if playing a game. The trees gradually began to change as they went deeper into the forest. The firs began to look a darker green and more recognisable, like the firs from their own time. Flowers, their colours so out of place, began to pop up in abundance interspersed beneath the trees, and the odd

Dragonfly buzzed past them. 'I wonder if they can speak?' thought Sam wishfully. Even the forest floor seemed to give off a feel of being alive, it's pine needles and moss-covered areas, springy to walk upon. Red mushrooms dotted with splashes of white dots grouped together in clusters.
The buzzing they had heard earlier was gradually increasing and Sam wondered if they were moving towards some piece of machinery, something that gave off this constant buzz they could all hear. Another boy, similarly dishevelled, suddenly appeared over a small rise. He stopped and looked at the other boy, then the three girls, before racing back the way he had come.
"Hey?" Jazz said loudly to the first boy, who stopped and looked at her, his face wearing a large smile. The buzzing was becoming increasingly louder and they all tensed, staffs at the ready when over the top of the rise, a moving mass of yellow and black swarmed into view.
Sam's eyes widened in shock, and then horror, when she saw the size of the Wasps. They were huge, each one at least a foot long. At first sight, it looked and sounded like a swarm but Sam counted just eight Wasps coming towards them, their black faceted eyes locked on the girls. She felt Thorfell grasp her collar and swing behind her. Sam thought back to her training, and remembered how she managed to focus on controlling the air around them, to push away the Bees. And then another thought raised its ugly face, causing her heart to beat faster. 'Chloe, if she gets stung by these Wasps without her EpiPen, it could be fatal!' She closed her eyes. 'Relax, Sam, focus, breath, take a deep breath and let it out slow. Focus on your task only, no distractions.'
She took a long slow breath in, a difficult task in itself in the circumstances, feeling the air filling her lungs, feeling her chest expand. A calm came over her as she opened her eyes, then her mouth, and let her breath out in one long slow exhale, seeing the colours of the air appearing like magic before her eyes. The Wasps were only yards away and heading directly at the group, when Sam held out her hands in front of her and focused on the air, her hands moving like a conductor, moving the rainbow colours up

and forward, forcing the Wasps to split and swerve past them in a deafening buzz, making the group all duck in a reflex action. As they buzzed past, so the size of the stingers, protruding from their yellow and black bodies, made Sam gulp. They were inches long and seemed to quiver and glisten in anticipation, the point looking as deadly as a rapier.

The Wasps banked and turned in a blur of speed, and headed back at the group with deadly intent. Sam whirled and took a few steps to stand in front of Chloe, before refocusing on the oncoming horde. She could feel her heart racing now, and was struggling to slow her mind down to concentrate, when a shrill whistle was heard. The Wasps paused instantly in mid-flight, hovering there, only a few yards from the group. Then the Wasps turned and disappeared into the branches, their buzzing lowering to a tolerable level as they flew away.

"That was close," Chloe said breathing heavily.

"You could say that," Jazz replied with a raise of an eyebrow. "Good skills, Sam," she added with a wink.

"Thank you," Sam replied, letting out a deep breath, "but that last bit wasn't my doing, it was his," she said pointing to a man silhouetted on top of the rise.

As they peered to look, so more figures appeared, standing behind the figure. All were of varying heights, but even from this distance, they could see that quite a few were children.

"Welcome," the man said with a deep voice. "Come, you have nothing to fear here," he beckoned.

"You could have fooled me," Chloe replied, "Those Wasps were about to attack us."

"Those 'Wasps', as you call them, are our friends. As long as you are with me, you have nothing to fear. Come," he said again, then turned and disappeared over the rise. A few others stayed on top, peering down at the girls until they started to follow, then they too moved off quickly. The buzzing increased again as they reached the crest of the rise, and stood on top looking down at an incredible sight.

Below them was a large clearing. One huge tree stood in the

middle, its branches sweeping far and wide above them, forming an umbrella like canopy. Light came through the thick green leaves, almost as if they didn't exist. But looking up, the girls could not see out, it was like a one-way prism, where daylight could filter through, but only in one direction. The light was the most beautiful Sam had ever seen, beams picked out people working in fields of flowers and different sorts of vegetation. Shadows from the branches gave a crisscross effect of shadow and light. A building had been erected from timber coming off the huge trunk, extending outwards to cover one whole side of the clearing. Everything seemed orderly and at peace. Children ran around the edges of the fields, playing and having fun, without a care in the world. Wasps flew in large numbers around the clearing, some landing on the flowers while others sat on the ground chewing on wood; with children playing around them. A line of circular holes, high up in the canopy was a hive of activity as Wasps came and went from their nests.

"This is unbelievable," Jazz said.

"It's beautiful," Chloe added, "apart from the Wasps, of course, they freak me out!"

"I never thought this could exist here, in this world," Sam said.

"That's the most beautiful tree I've ever seen," Thorfell said, appearing from behind Sam's shoulder.

"You realise, that if we are successful, this will never come to be," Jazz added solemnly.

Their four sets of eyes met and an understanding of what this meant suddenly dawned on them all.

"We must move on, right away, we cannot stop here," Sam said nervously.

"I agree," squeaked Thorfell.

"I think it's too late for that, Sam," Jazz said, nodding her head towards the man who was approaching them.

"Ah, good, so you decided to join us, welcome, my name is Lorofax, I am the Guardian here."

"Guardian?" Jazz exclaimed.

"Guardian?" Sam repeated.

The man was huge, at least six foot, big boned and barrel chested. He stood leaning on a staff that had a blue stone attached to the top that was held in place by an intricately carved hand. A long messy brown beard with hints of grey showed a little of his age. A large red squashed nose sat below his bushy eyebrows. Deep brown eyes peered at them with warmth, but at the same time with a hint of quizzicality. A smile that formed wrinkles on his leathery tanned face, showed a set of stained white teeth. He frowned at the girls' questions.

"I am the Guardian of this place," he said raising his arms wide, "I look after and care for the Humans that come to live here."

"Here? What is 'here'?" Jazz asked.

"Perhaps you should introduce yourselves first?" he said with a wry smile.

"I'm sorry, it's been a long day already," Sam interrupted Jazz, "My name is Sam, this is Jazz and Chloe," she said pointing to them, and they waved at him. "And this is Thorfell," she added looking over her shoulder at him, "he's a Pixie."

"My oh my, a Pixie, I have never seen one of those," he said walking up to Sam and peering down closely to look at Thorfell with a wry smile.

"Pleased to meet you," Thorfell squeaked, making the big man take an involuntary step back, before bringing out a nervous laugh. "My oh my," he said again, under his breath.

Just then, something passed over the canopy, it's shadow racing across the forest floor like a black tide. The shadow was recognisable to all. Everyone stopped and peered upwards, a sudden feeling of fear sweeping through them. Lorofax put a finger to his mouth to warn the girls to be still. Only the Wasps moved, they flew upwards to hover just beneath the canopy, only just visible as they were so high up. Like a squadron of fighter planes, they followed the flight of the Dragon, as if ready to attack it. The shadow disappeared and then returned, flying in the opposite direction. A few more seconds drifted by slowly, and then Lorofax relaxed and turned to the people who were all looking at him expectantly. He clapped his hands once and they all turned and resumed their activities. The Wasps returned to their duties, and all seemed to be at peace again.

"Have some drinks with me and I will explain things a little. And I have many questions myself."

They followed him, and entered a single-storey building built from wood and with open windows. The longest table they had ever seen greeted their wide-eyed stares, it stretched from the doorway for at least fifty yards into the trunk.

"We built this from one of the roots," he said smiling, seeing their amazement.

"Before we continue, for the security of the swarm, I need to know who you are, please? You somehow deflected my friends away from you, which was impressive, do you have some sort of magic? There Is very little magic left in this world, but in you three I sense Earth magic. It flows around you, unseen to the eye, but for those that can see, it is there. And in so doing, you have endangered our home."

'Of course,' thought Sam, 'as soon as I used the magic, it became a beacon to Moribund and his followers! Why did I not think of that?' she chastised herself.

Her mind was racing now. 'Swarm? Earth magic? Could Guinevere have something to do with this?'

"We have come from a distant place and are trying to get home. We need to get to the hole in the rock in the bay, and pass through that. Our magic can return us home. We have some sick friends who need our help, so time is against us," Jazz said tight lipped and as confidently as she could. Lorofax looked at them for a few moments as if weighing up the conversation, then turned and reached for some cups.

Over drinks, created from honey, water and plant extract, and some food which seemed to revitalise them no end, Lorofax told them his story, which was both beautiful and horrific, and left the four dumbstruck for some minutes after he had finished.

"These Humans you see are all the ones that have escaped the camps. I find them, bring them here, and if they wish to stay, then this can become there home. I have been doing this for many,

many years, as my predecessor did before me and his also. But our numbers are dropping, we do not have enough to sustain a colony, it is only a matter of time, a few decades perhaps ..." he trailed off, leaving the sentence unfinished. He looked away for the briefest of moments when he said this, and Sam looked at him, thinking that some part of this did not ring true.

"You've noticed that they do not speak. That is because they cannot. In the camps, they cut out the tongues of the newborn to stop us talking, but we have found a new way to communicate here," he said with a grimace. The girls looked at each other, eyes wide in horror.

"Telepathy," Sam said.

"Yes, if that is what you call it. We call it simply 'mind talk'. We think the name or names first, to start the conversation, and everyone else switches off; it is a great gift that we have learned over the centuries."

"And the Wasps?" Chloe asked.

"Wasps?"

"Yes, the big yellow and black flying killing machines?" she added.

"Ah, we do not know of them as Wasps, that does not sound like a nice name, it sounds aggressive. Here we simply call them, our clever little flying friends. Over many years we have evolved a symbiotic relationship with our clever little flying friends. They provide us protection and honey, and we produce the flowers that keep them alive. It works very well. They are beautiful creatures, so gentle, all they want is to survive and protect their swarm, and of course, we are part of that swarm now. They are brave and loyal, and very powerful. You know, I have never seen another creature alive, outside of this forest, apart from the horrors that run this world and the Human slaves."

"You said protection, protection from what?"

"Why, the Dragons of course. Our clever little flying friends could knock out a Dragon with just a few stings. It is one of the few things the Dragon's fear. When I go out searching, a few always accompany me. That's why we are safe in here, they would not dare come near here, they know what the outcome would be.

However, it does seem strange that they flew over just as you arrived?" he said, lowering his chin and lifting one hand to play with his beard. Again, he looked at them for a few moments in silence, his thoughts his own. "Come, let me show you around," he said suddenly, leading them out of the building, through the fields and towards an opening in the trees they had not seen before. He stopped and turned back to face them.
"Why are you really here?" Lorofax asked, his look pensive.
"We're here to put things right ..." Chloe started to say, then stopped, realising she had let on too much. Her mouth clamped shut like a crocodile.
"To put things right," he repeated. "What do you mean by that?" he asked, seeing the three Guardians' nervous looks.
"We need to escape this realm, to return to our time ..." Jazz explained, looking Lorofax in the eye.
"To put things right," he stated again.
"Look, we just want to get home," Sam said. "to our families, to save our friends. Going through that stone is the only way back, that is our only chance."
Lorofax looked at them for what seemed like an age. Sam tried to hold his gaze, her eyes unblinking. He played with his unruly beard in one hand, while the index finger on his other hand tapped away on the tip of his staff. Each tap a heartbeat of thought, as if it were the drum beat of doom for those being led to the gallows. Sam became fixated on the hand and the jewelled knob of wood on the staff that Lorofax held. The blue light that emanated from it was unearthly and cold, unlike the feeling that Sam felt for this kind man before her. 'Was he deciding what to do with them?' She sensed the Wasps, pausing in their tasks, feeling their black eyes looking at them, waiting for Lorafax to decide their fate.
He took in a deep breath, his decision made. "Very well. We will help you as much as we can, but I will not endanger my people or the 'Wasps 'as you call them. Our survival and the ecology here, depends on both to survive. Without one, the other would wither and die."
"We understand," Jazz replied. "We do not want anyone to get

harmed either, we just want to return home."

"Yes, you must tell me more about your home, I would be interested to know what it is like?" he asked, his deep mellow tone sounding inquisitive. "Come, we will eat and you can tell me more," he said, clapping his huge shovel hands twice.

Everyone in the clearing stopped as one, and looked up before downing tools and walking towards the large seating area, a mix of smiles and silent conversation following the groups back to the building. The Wasps, as if in sync rose and flew towards their nests, the loud humming still sending shivers of fear down Sam's spine.

When the last Human had entered the eating area, Lorofax looked around to check that everyone, including the wasps, had left the clearing. Then he turned back towards the Guardians, his face a grimace of anger, his eyes wide, his lips pinched.

"Do you take me for a fool?" he asked quietly. "I might be running this place, but it doesn't mean I am in control. If they sense you are a threat to this community, they will kill you and there will be nothing I can do to stop them ... The truth now, please?"

Sam looked at her friends, her mind reeling, then took a deep breath. 'Tell him the truth,' she told herself. "We are going home to make this right ... this world, this realm ... shouldn't be. A man called Moribund stole something from us and went back in time, and changed history to," she spread her hand out, "this. This world shouldn't exist. Humans rule the world where we come from. There are no Dragons. Skree and Erlking are banished beneath the Earth. Humans aren't slaves to them, we are free."

"It's a beautiful place, compared to this," Chloe added.

"So, you plan on getting the thing this person stole, and do what?"

"Change history back to what it should be," Chloe said before realising what that would mean.

Lorofax shot a stare at Chloe. "And what is going to happen to this world, our realm? This is our home, we live here. Despite what you see, this is how we have learnt to survive in this world. If you change history, do we just cease to exist? Is that what happens?"

"If we don't try, millions will die." Jazz replied.

"From what you are saying, those millions never existed in the first place, not here, so no one will die," Lorafax argued.

"They have in our realm, our timeline, they have been wiped out of existence as if they never existed, but they did, otherwise we wouldn't be here at all. We've lost everything, our parents, our families, friends, everything…"

"This world should not be. Moribund has changed it to his liking and destroyed it. He destroyed my realm too. The Earth is dying and it's only a matter of time before you are captured or killed, it cannot last, you've told us that they hunt you, that the magic is nearly gone, that your numbers are dwindling. You cannot sustain this existence for much longer, you know that, deep down." Thorfell said, from on top of Sam's shoulder.

"Lorofax, this is not how the world should be. Please, listen to the Guardians, help us if you can."

Lorofax stared at Thorfell, then glanced back towards the eating area, then up into the trees before returning his gaze to the three Guardians. "If I help you, I am sealing all of these people to our doom," he said, shaking his head.

"If we don't succeed, our realm will never exist and in this world, we will all be doomed," Jazz replied sharply, then added. "Moribund would have won."

"I cannot help, I am sorry, I cannot be a part of destroying my own world, you ask too much of me," he paused looking down at the earth, his foot working some loose soil back into place. "You must leave now. Go, before I change my mind, please leave," he said pointing. "We will not hinder you on your journey, but neither will we help you, it is not right to work so willingly to orchestrate your own downfall, and the death of all you hold dear … even if you say it is for the greater good," he turned and walked back towards the long table.

The girls looked at each other for the briefest of moments, shaken by the unexpected turn of events that had taken place.

"We need to go, now," said Jazz, breaking the stunned silence.

Without another word, they picked up their belongings and headed off up a well-worn track towards the sea, and a destiny that they wished to influence.

CHAPTER 4 - THE THURLE STONE

They reached the river in minutes and were amazed to see a rope bridge going from one side to the other, across the narrowest point, covered and camouflaged entirely by the leaves of the great tree. Because of the slight bottleneck as the river narrowed, the water seemed to be moving faster, causing eddies and making more noise. The bridge was rocking in the slight breeze, but looked sturdy enough and was obviously well used. The day was starting to turn to night now, and the shadows from the trees on the opposite bank looked dark and foreboding. The bridge hung at least twenty feet above the river and stretched across the water for about fifty yards, into the shadows on the other side. As one, they looked downriver to see the island where the Dragons nest was, and saw no sign of them.

"Where are they?" Sam asked, peering into the sky for any sign.

"Shall we wait until dark to cross?" Chloe said.

"I think it's safe now, we need to keep moving," Jazz replied.

"Perhaps we should cross one at a time?" Sam questioned.

"So, if one of us gets frazzled, the others might get through!" Chloe chortled.

"Something like that," Sam replied with a frown.

"We go together, remember," Jazz said, looking upriver then down again, as if she was learning the green cross code. "Let's go."

Jazz led the way, putting one step on the first rung, while gripping the rope support for balance. The spaces between the foot supports were small and there was no chance of falling through, and the timber was solid. She looked back, gave a thumbs up with her free hand and marched across with a confident stride. Chloe followed close behind, with Sam bringing up the rear. With each step as they moved out of the shadows of the overhanging trees into the dim evening light, so they felt more and more exposed. Despite the canopy covering, Sam felt more nervous than she had felt all day. She peered down at the river and became almost hypnotised by the strong steady flow of the water. The water looked deep and dark, and threatening. They were halfway across and moving fast, when around the bend in the river, a Dragon appeared, its wing tips almost touching both sides of the forest as it glided barely a few feet above the surface, its movements causing eddies in the river. Within seconds, it would be upon them. For the briefest of moments, it took Sam back to Burrator and the Dragon that had nearly been reborn out of the waters of the reservoir, and then panic set in. Wide eyed, she realised that they were too far away from safety in front of them and had no time to return back either, they were trapped in the open.

"Guardians, stay where you are and stay still," a voice said in her head, Lorofax. *"It cannot see you if you are stationary. Trust me."*

The three looked at each other, then towards the approaching Dragon. It was so close they didn't have time to move even if they had wanted to. It seemed as if it was going to crash right through the bridge and throw them into the water below. But at the last minute it lifted its long scaly neck, kicked with its legs, and flapped its great wings once to help it rise above the bridge. The Dragon was so close that they could have reached up and touched it. An acrid smell of brimstone followed in its wake. Its tail swished, swirling in rhythm with the body, catching a tiny part of the canopy as it flew over. A segment of the covering was lifted clean off, to clatter down around them. The bridge swung menacingly to-and-fro, and the three gripped tight to the rope holds trying not to move. The Dragon, hearing the commotion, turned its head in flight and seemed to peer right at them, one snakelike eye contracting as it spied the three humans.

"Run," Jazz shouted and moved. Chloe charged after her, letting go of the rope so she could move faster. Sam did the same, nearly lost her balance, then seeing the Dragon out of the corner of her eye starting to rise above the trees so it could turn back towards them, she regained her balance and ran across the bridge as fast as

she could, letting her momentum keep her upright. The Dragon rose above the tops of the trees, swivelled in a wide arc, and shot back towards the bridge, the long slow beats of its wings belittling the speed of its travel.
Jazz reached the other side first and turned to help, and was almost bundled over by Chloe.
"Keep going," she shouted, pushing her friend in front of her.
Sam was only two paces behind when a roar, like they had never heard before, erupted from behind them. She kept running not peering back until they were a good distance into the trees. They turned, protecting themselves behind some large trunks and looked back. The bridge was on fire now. The Dragon had spurted its deadly charge upon the bridge thinking that they were still upon it. Fire raced up and down its length, as the Dragon passed over again breathing another plume of fire from its snout, hitting the bridge full on in a different place this time. The wood and leaf canopy erupted in flames and the rope crackled and snapped as large chunks of the bridge fell sizzling into the river, and were swept out to sea. After barely a few minutes the bridge was gone. The Dragon swept along the river barely a few feet above the water, its grey snout peering downwards into the depths for any sign of the Humans it was hunting. After one final pass, it lifted itself above the trees and was gone.
"This has been one long day!" Chloe said with a smile of relief.
"Chloe, I think that's the biggest understatement of your life," Jazz replied.
Sam sat down with her back against a trunk, her legs aching from the run, and let out a long slow sigh of relief. "We need to rest. We can't go on without one, we are all knackered!"
"I'll second that!" Chloe replied, falling to one knee on the forest floor, "That was one close call," she added, hardly believing what had just happened.
"I agree, we need to rest, let's head in a bit further, find somewhere that looks safe and take it in turns to sleep. We can head out at first light, get to the Thurle Stone and sort this mess out," Jazz said.
"Mess, now that's definitely an understatement of the highest

order," Chloe said with a chuckle. "Sorting out this mess by going forward in time and back in time to change history to save all of Humanity, is definitely understated by calling it a mess. It's definitely tiring work though, I'm exhausted and hungry too!"
"We can eat when we find a decent place to rest," Jazz added.
"Who put you in charge?" Chloe asked, with a wink at Sam.
They walked through the forest until they came to a small clearing, beside a stream that was sheltered by some overhanging trees. They crept under the low branches, and sat down with their backs to the trunks, the stream in front of them. They decided to take it in turns to sleep, always leaving one of them on watch. Thorfell took the first watch, and after all that had happened that day, Sam, Jazz and Chloe were soon fast asleep.

"That doesn't look good!" Chloe said quietly.
They were standing under the overhang of the trees, looking down towards a crescent shaped beach and headland. The forest stopped at the edge of a cliff to their right, and to a line of burnt trees in front of them. From there on, the land was scorched black and bare for as far as the eye could see. The occasional gorse bush, its yellow buds standing out in the dawn light, clung to life within the desolate landscape, as if bursting through from beneath the earth to show that not all was dead and burnt to dust. The land swung down before them and up to the closest headland before continuing around the bay to the farthest headland that was visible. In the bay, stood their goal, the Thurle stone and a chance to return home. Unfortunately for the three Guardians and Thorfell, a Dragon's nest sat atop the closest headland that was directly overlooking the stone.
"That sucks!" Chloe added.
The night had passed quickly with each of the girls getting about four hours sleep each as they rotated watch. Sam had fallen almost immediately into a long deep sleep that even the events of the day could not intrude upon. She had awoken feeling in-

credibly fresh and revitalised. The others felt the same, the sleep giving them renewed energy and a new found belief that they were close to achieving their goal. That was until they reached the edge of the forest and looked down at the scene before them. Two huge Dragons rested together upon the headland, both facing out to sea. They seemed to be sleeping, but the odd flick of their tails or movement of a wing, denoted that they were not in a deep sleep. Whether one of these was the one that destroyed the bridge, they could not tell, but they all knew the destruction these creatures could wreak.

They had watched long enough to know that the tide was just starting to come in. A series of rocks protruded from the sea, covered in green and brown seaweed, led all the way to the stone. As the tide was rising, so they could see that water was already surrounding the stone, giving them the feeling that this would be even trickier than just avoiding the interest of the Dragons. The hole itself was already partly submerged, and would gradually disappear as the tide rose.

The day was grey with the sun hiding behind a low bank of clouds, casting a monochrome filter over the whole scene. A fine sea mist drifted in and out, like the gentle waves that lapped upon the beach. A deathly silence seemed to hang over the place as if the air itself was holding its breath.

Sam gulped, the sound feeling loud in her own mind. She looked at the beach, the cliffs below the Dragons and the rocks that led out to the rock. If they could get to those cliffs undetected, they could climb out most of the way unseen. It would only be the last few yards and final swim to get around the stone three times and then through, where they would be exposed. And then she thought of the Creature of the Depths she had sensed when she was in the cavern, and a shudder went through her body. 'We will stick to the rocks as much as we can, 'she thought, with a little panic in her mind. They needed a distraction but couldn't think of anything. Thorfell offered to be bait but the girls would have nothing of that, they were going to stick together whatever happened.

As time was rushing by, they set out at a quick pace through the trees towards the furthest point they could get to before leaving the cover of the forest. Standing behind the last line of trees they all turned to each other, fear and anxiety causing shallow lines to form on their young faces. The Dragons nest was less than two hundred yards from them now, and they could hear the loud snorting noise of the pair, above the sound of the waves on the beach.

"It's now or never!" Jazz said, tight lipped.

"Yep," Sam replied, dry mouthed.

"To infinity and ..." Chloe started, then saw her friends wide-eyed stares of disapproval. "Sorry, just a bit nervous, I'm not keen on getting frazzled. I never liked the History lesson about Joan of Arc, that always upset me, for some reason. Now, I know why!"

"We are not going to be seen, we are going to get home," Jazz replied with a confidence she didn't feel.

"OK, let's do it," Chloe replied, starting forward. Ahead of them, the tree line stopped on the sharp edge of the cliff, as if the land had been carved out with a huge knife. A short drop to the beach and they could then keep undercover of the overhang of the cliff all the way to the rocks. With one final look to her left, Chloe crept forward and leant over, using the roots of a tree that had been exposed by a landfall to help her over the edge. She hung for the briefest of moments, then let go and disappeared. The two remaining Guardians peered towards the nest, nothing moved. Letting out a deep sigh, Sam told Thorfell to hold tight, and followed Chloe's lead. As she hung off the edge, she took a quick look down to see that Chloe wasn't in the way, then let go and dropped the short distance to the sand. Righting herself, she stepped under the overhang and pushed herself against the rock face. A tap of approval from Chloe helped her breathe out and relax a little. Jazz dropped silently into the sand moments later, and followed suit. She rose and moved under the overhang, brushing herself off. For the briefest of seconds, they looked at each other, listening for any disturbance, then moved on, hugging the cliff face, heading towards the outcrop of rocks on the other side of the beach.

To Sam, now that the Dragons were out of sight, it felt far worse not knowing what they were up to. They could be right above them and they wouldn't even know. Tension gripped her, fear causing her muscles to tighten, her mind playing tricks with every sound or movement until she was ready to scream. She wanted to shout at the sea to stop the noise of the tide, but inwardly laughed at the thought; which somehow gave her a sense of gravity. Her hands felt clammy and cold, the staff, slippery in her hand.
"Relax," Thorfell whispered in her ear, trying to calm her. "Use your training to calm yourself."
She took a breath and let it out, then a longer slower one, feeling her heart starting to slow. She closed her eyes momentarily and opened them to see the colours of the wind all around her. The sight was beautiful. With the sea and tide and winds, the rainbow effects crisis crossed and moved, as if alive. She smiled.
"Thanks, Thorfell."
"You're welcome."
They came to a point in the middle of the beach where the cliff had collapsed, which they had not seen from the trees. By now, the trees were far behind them and only scorched earth that smelled acrid and gave no concealment, met their gaze at the edge of the cliff face. The Dragons were barely fifty yards away, the rocks agonisingly close. The tide was continuing to come in, at what seemed like an alarming rate.
'We are running out of time!' Sam thought.
Peering around the edge, Sam could see the snout of one Dragon leaning over the edge of the cliff and it reminded her of her old dog, who used to sit on top of the landing and rest its head over the edge. Only her dog didn't have a six foot snout with two sets of razor sharp teeth, and the ability to breath fire.
Together, they crossed the open space as fast as they could, all of them looking up towards the Dragon's head for any sign of movement. They pulled in close to the cliff with the Dragon's snout still visible about fifty feet directly above them. They were all breathing fast. Chloe put her thumb up with a forced smile. Ten-

sion hung in the air like the fine mist that seemed to drift in and out with the tide, in rhythmic fashion. One minute the rocks and stone were clear to see, a minute later and it would be smudged almost out of sight completely. 'If we could time it right, 'Sam thought.
Jazz lifted her foot and pointed to it, then the sand. 'Their footsteps! Oh no, would the dragons see them?' Sam thought in panic. They were just about to move when something struck Chloe on the head and shoulders covering her in a slimy clear mess. They all looked up and quickly shuffled out of the way.
Chloe looked wide eyed and disgusted, then moved in close to whisper to them.
"I don't believe it, I've just been splattered in Dragon drool! Brilliant! And don't even say it's good luck, like having bird poo land on you…"
Despite the gravity of the situation, Sam and Jazz put their hand's to their mouth's to stop themselves from laughing out loud. Sam snorted and took a few deep breaths to gather herself. Jazz shook her head and started off, the others quickly following. They moved past the Dragons and stood facing the rocks that led out to the Thurle stone. Everyone glimpsed back and upwards. No movement came from above. A line of taller grey coloured rocks, covered in sea urchins and barnacles, which was tall enough to conceal them, stretched out into the sea. They slipped behind the natural cover, crouching low and shuffling forwards until they reached where the waves were lapping against the rocks. The Thurle Stone now loomed ever closer, its size larger than Sam had at first thought. A loud snort from a Dragon brought them to their senses, making them dive for cover behind the nearest rock. The sharp edge of the rocks dug into their palms as they glimpsed, through a crack, to see one of the Dragons starting to rise. It flapped its wings and shook its body as if shaking off sleep. Its neck stretched out and up, and it rose onto its four trunklike legs. It stood there for a while looking out to sea, its gaze seemingly scanning the horizon. One final shake of its snout and it turned and disappeared from view. The other Dragon turned and

stretched but stayed lying down, its snout only just visible on the cliff top.

Water was lapping around their ankles now and Sam could feel the cold and damp seeping through her shoes and socks. A salty smell hung in the air, and it took Sam back in time to the many occasions that they had visited this beach in the last few years. Their clothes were already wet and damp from the mist and Sam could feel herself beginning to shake, and wondered whether it was from the cold or fear?

"It's now or never," Jazz said. "We head for that large outcrop of rocks and gather behind there before moving on," she said dry mouthed. Behind that outcrop stood a little open sea and in the middle of it, the Thurle Stone itself.

She broke cover, climbing fast over the rocks with an assured step towards the larger outcrop. Chloe started off, her natural agility helping her to pass Jazz and carry on. Rock pools with small crabs and silver fish, which darted off behind some coral as soon as they neared, dotted the rocks forcing them to divert left and right, making the going agonisingly slow. Green and brown seaweed covered some rocks and this they tried to avoid, knowing too well how slippery that would be. They were completely exposed now. If the Dragons looked their way, they would be spotted immediately. Sam paused behind Jazz and looked back momentarily, her heart pumping fast. The second Dragon was now starting to stir, she could see it starting to rise. She turned back to Jazz, her hands touching her back. Out of the corner of her eyes, she watched Chloe leap across a chasm and land with both feet on the opposite rock face while reaching out both hands for purchase, and finding it. In seconds she was up and over the top, behind the outcrop and undercover.

Before them, a six foot wide chasm dropped some twenty feet to the sea below. Waves lapped against the rocks, the noise covering their passage, the tide showing that the sea was deep at this point.

"I can't make that," Jazz said in fear.
"Course you can, Jazz," Sam said nonchalantly, "if Chloe can do it,

so can you."

"I can't make that," she repeated, her body frozen in fear.

"Jazz, the Dragon is ..."

A loud roar went up behind them. Sam and Jazz turned to see the Dragon staring directly at them, its huge mouth open as another roar erupted from its throat. The sound seemed to echo around the beach and through the mist, like some ancient fog horn. They both stared wide-eyed as the first Dragon appeared in the air above the second, its eyes spotting the movement of the two Guardians instantly. A second later it dove over the cliff and swooped down towards them.

Jazz turned and without hesitation, took one step forward and jumped. As if in slow motion, Sam watched as Jazz crossed the chasm and got both feet on the rocks, while reaching up with both hands, one still clutching the staff. Her fingers gripped the rocks with relief even as her left foot slipped and came off the rocks, her weight pulling her down. The hand holding the staff also came off and with hardly anything holding her up, she slipped and fell.

"Jazz ..." Sam screamed, as she watched Jazz drop towards the sea. As she fell, her head struck an outcrop and her body went limp as it hit the water and sank beneath the waves like a stone.

"Jazz," Sam screamed again. "Hold tight, Thorfell," she said and jumped off and out.

Chloe hearing the commotion raced back up to the top of the rock face and reached the top just as the Dragon appeared above the rocks. She froze having not even known that the Dragon was coming. It swooped towards her as she stood completely stationary locked in fear, watching as her doom neared. She didn't have time to move but her muscles had locked as she saw the huge Dragon hurtle towards her, it's eyes seemingly fixed on her. The Dragon paused in mid-flight its wings spreading wide to halt its progress, then hovered there, its snout only ten feet from Chloe. Chloe felt herself starting to shake as the Dragon opened its snout, closed it again, then sniffed the air. It sniffed again, hardly believing what it could sense. Its sense of smell and hearing far outweighed its relatively poor eyesight. It sniffed the air for the Humans it had spotted moving on the rocks, but now nothing moved and it could not smell any Human. In fact, the only scent was that of another Dragon, its mate who sat atop the cliff also watching for any movement. Its small brain couldn't comprehend, and its senses were what kept it alive and safe and they were never wrong.

Chloe stood motionless still but her brain was starting to put things together. She let out a very long slow breath and braced herself, her thoughts of escape returning. 'The Dragon drool is covering my natural scent, it can't see me as long as I stay still,' she thought. She wanted to leap for joy, but thought better of it. 'Perhaps it is good luck after all! 'she thought as her mind then turned to her friends.

Even as she saw the Dragon turn and begin to flap its wings to fly off so Sam's head suddenly appeared above the waves, her arms around a motionless Jazz. They had been dragged out to sea by the undertow and were actually closer to the Thurle stone, but Chloe could see that she was struggling.

"Help," Sam shouted.

The Dragon snapped its head back and seemed to twist in midair, its body somehow magically rolling and turning back at the sound of Sam's scream. Chloe, who was no longer in the Dragon's eye line, darted back over the rock face and made her way as quickly as she could along the rocks towards Sam, Jazz and the hole in the rock. She reached the edge of the rock and looked down into the water towards her friends.

Sam held Jazz's unconscious body between her and her left arm, that held her staff. With the other hand she paddled weakly and kicked with her legs beneath the surface to stay afloat. The pull of the tide was stronger than she thought and it was tugging her, more and more, out to sea. Miraculously Jazz somehow had her arms entangled around her staff which bobbed up and down in the water beside her. The water was full of brown seaweed and Sam was panicking that her feet would get entangled, and she would be pulled down. She was shaking from the cold, her clothes heavy and dragging her down. Her eyes stung with the salt and through her blurred vision she looked up, her head and Jazz's just

above the water line, to see a giant form blank out the light of the day as it hovered a few feet above the water peering down at them. Jazz suddenly coughed and started to come too, squirming in Sam's arms and breaking free, only to sink beneath the surface.
"No," she screamed, swallowing water as she sank down to reach for Jazz.
"I've got her," a voice said from beside Sam. Chloe dragged Jazz up above the water, her own body slipping beneath the surface momentarily. Jazz coughed up water, opened her eyes and stared wide eyed at the Dragon that hung above their position.
"Thorfell," Sam spluttered.
"I'm here," he said from beside her left ear.
"I hope you can hold your breath?" she said.
"I have been, already!" he replied.
"Yes, of course. Jazz, you OK."
"My head hurts, but I'm OK, thanks," she said to the two of them.
"I'm OK," Chloe added, and they all smiled weakly.
They floated there, all three embracing, supporting each other in the sea, treading water, once more staring up at the Dragon. The Dragon hovered there, its wings swishing slowly up and back, holding its position. Its senses were still playing tricks with it. Something was in the sea, but with all the movements of the seaweed and the smell and sounds of the sea, it wasn't sure what it was. But twice now it had sensed movement, so to be sure, it would vent its rage in the only way it knew. Its mouth began to open and they all looked up in horror, past the rows of dirty sharp teeth to see a tiny flame of light ignite within the back of its throat.

CHAPTER 5 – DRAGONS END

Standing under the overhang of the line of burnt out trees, Lorofax watched the scene unfold, his face impassive. Using his staff as support, he felt his pulse beating fast with the turmoil that was raging between his head and his heart. The Guardians had not recognised him, he thought. How could they? And to see his beloved again. That had been a hard secret to live with, one that hung heavy in his heart. Although their powers were strong, they still had not fully encompassed what they were or what they could become, but they would never know if he did not act. But what would become of this world, his family, his flying friends? For himself, he was only sad, he had been sent on a quest a long time ago and this was what he was here for. If he succeeded then he could at least die happy. And despite the time and what he had achieved in this world, his quest had not changed. "Protect the Guardians, at all costs! Nothing else matters," his King had said so long ago. He had been sent here for this one sole purpose. His mission as a Knight of the Round Table was straight forward at the time and demanded the ultimate sacrifice, which he had willingly accepted to clear his name and restore his honour. Could he fail his King again?

"No," he said aloud, "I will not fail Arthur again. I am a Knight of the Round Table and I will not let this happen." As he spoke, so he lowered his head, closed his eyes and the light on the end of his staff began to pulse in a faster quicker rhythm.

"Dive!" Chloe screamed above the sound of the sea and the noise of the Dragon's wings.

"I don't know how to!" Jazz said, wide eyed in fear.

They could see the fire igniting within the Dragon's mouth, its eyes fixed on the spot where they were. With its head tilted back and up they sensed that the Dragon was about to throw its head forward and shoot out a spurt of fire, when suddenly something struck it in the side of the neck, jolting it and causing it to use it wings more to stay in position. Something else thudded into its side, causing the Dragon to bellow, its great wings lifting it effortlessly into the sky. The cry was one of fright mixed with anger, as the Dragon turned its great head to see what had caused it to lose its position. A Wasp struck it in the neck and it bellowed again as the stinger found the soft flesh between its scales. More came at its head and it snapped its jaws tight on them even as one of the Wasps sank its tail into the softness of its mouth. It bellowed again, an almost sad cry of hopelessness as it peered back towards its nest for help, its mind already succumbing to the poison. Its wings felt heavy, the muscles failing to work, the weight of its torso and dying heart within, making the Dragon drop towards the ocean like a stone. More Wasps darted in, their stingers bending forward to inflict agony upon the hapless Dragon, even as it fell.

"Hurry, make your way to the stone," Lorofax's voice said in their heads.

"Come on," Sam said, with renewed purpose, swimming towards the Thurle Stone. By now the tide had risen and was already covering half the stone with the hole now barely visible above the waves. They were within touching distance when there was a loud crash, as the Dragon plummeted into the sea barely twenty yards behind them. It floated on top for a few moments, the Wasps hovering above it in formation, before it sank without trace into the depths of the bay.

Another roar went up as the second Dragon dropped off the cliff, fire spewing from its mouth in a wide arc, to destroy the Wasps coming towards it.

"Hurry!" Sam screamed as the three reached the rock and began to swim around it. One circuit down and the Dragon turned its head towards them, its eyes sensing movement in the water. More Wasps approached it and it sprayed them with another volley of fire. Some ducked and dived and managed to get though, one finding the soft flesh on its hind leg before it was swatted away. Another stuck to its wing and tried to pierce its thin hide, but only succeeded in ripping a tiny hole in its thin leathery vein like flesh. By now, most of the Wasps were dead or dying, and only a few remained. They hung there in the air, facing the oncoming Dragon like gunslingers of the Wild West. The Guardians could hear the faint buzzing of the Wasps, even from where they were. Two circuits down and the Dragon sprayed another volley of fire. All but one of the Wasps moved out of the way in time, spreading and coming at the Dragon from different directions.

Sam was tiring and she could sense Thorfell struggling to hold on, but she couldn't stop. The hole was nearly gone, with only a few inches visible above the surface.

Out of the corner of her eye, she watched in amazement as the Dragon twisted in mid-air while firing a volley of short sharp fire bolts that took out the last of the Wasps, leaving the way clear for it to attack them. It swooped forward and with two giant flaps of its huge wings, bore down on them with alarming speed.

'We're not going to make it,' she thought in fright as she finished the third circuit, and treading water faced the submerged hole.

Chloe joined her and they both looked back towards Jazz who was still on the other side of the rock and working her way around slowly. Jazz had always been the weakest swimmer of the three, and had given up the classes before them, not liking it as much as Chloe and Sam. In all the confusion, Sam had forgotten this and now it could cost them their lives.

"I've got a plan," Chloe said spluttering water.

"What sort of plan?" Sam asked struggling to stay afloat and feeling Thorfell pull himself upright on her shoulder while staring wide eyed in fear at the oncoming behemoth.

"A plan that will give us all enough time to get through. You need to pull Jazz down and through. You trust me, right?"

"Yes, yes, of course."

"Then watch this," Chloe said and put her face beneath the waves for the briefest of moments.

"Chloe, what are you ..."

The Dragon reached them as Jazz came around the rock and headed towards Sam, Chloe and Thorfell, her head going from side to side with the effort of swimming. The Dragon slowed, swept over them and alighted upon the remaining rock of the Thurle stone, and peered down from a few yards away, as if it were a cat looking at goldfish in a pond. Its giant clawed front legs grasped the rock in an iron grip, its sharp clawed talons stretching under the water to cover a part of the hole. Its tail swished in the sea behind it like a coiled sea serpent.

Jazz reached Sam and straightened up, treading water then looked up in shock at the Dragon sitting atop the rock. Waves lapped over the top of the rock, and across the Dragon's legs.

Before the Dragon could do anything, something erupted out of the water and pounced on its snout. Chloe's shadowchaser ripped at the Dragon's eyes and snout. The Dragon bellowed and fell off its perch falling into the water behind the rock. As it fell, so it's front talons ripped shards of rock off the top of the stone, causing a crack to form in the rock.

"Quick," Chloe shouted, diving under the water and disappearing.

"I can't dive," Jazz said again as Sam grasped her, pushed her in front of her and said.

"Hold your breath."

She dived gripping Jazz in one hand, pulling her down and kicking towards the hole. Under the water, the visibility was murky, but she could see the opening only a few feet in front of her when a taloned hand shot down inches from her face. She swerved, pulled Jazz to the left of the reaching talon and swam through the hole in the rock.

Everything changed in an instant. Sam tumbled forward, no longer being kept upright by the water and knocked into Jazz, bowling her over and into Chloe who caught Jazz in her outstretched arms. Sam righted herself, feeling solid rock beneath her feet, then looked around.

"We are back to beneath the Tor!" Chloe exclaimed looking up.

"We're not even wet," Jazz exclaimed. "We need to move, before

we meet ourselves," she added her eyes wide, a frown upon her face. Already a bump was forming on her forehead. The bump was covered in a line of scratches formed by the rock she had struck, but she seemed no worse for wear.
"Cool," Chloe said, touching her clothes, feeling how dry they were.
"We have to find this Tristan and get this weapon for Lancelot, so we can stop this once and for all." Jazz said.
"And then can we have a rest!" Chloe exclaimed.
"Not yet you can't," Jazz replied with a wink. "Come on, we can't stay here."
They could hear the sounds of battle coming from above them. To Sam, it was an eerie feeling looking up those steps that led to the battlements, knowing full well that soon another version of themselves would be appearing there and heading up the circular opening towards a meeting with King Arthur and Moribund.
With one final glance behind her Jazz turned and entered the tunnel just as four familiar looking figures appeared and stood there looking up towards the battlements, each with an expression of disbelief.
They raced through the tunnel on tired legs and came out into the cavern with the underground river on their right, and the rows of stalagmites and stalactites in front of them. They made their way through this and entered the opposite tunnel through the door that had been left open. Tiredness and aching limbs slowed them down, but determination to succeed drove their young bodies forward. Sam didn't want to think about what would happen to Lorofax and his clan if they were successful, she could not come to terms with the thought at all and banished it to the back of her mind, focussing instead on what must be done.
They came to the end of the tunnel, passing the place where they knew King Arthur would fall into his deep sleep and spotted a thin line of stairs that led up to a door in the wall, some twenty feet above them. They made their way up and stood huddled together, Sam's hand on the ornate wooden handle. Behind the door, they could hear the sound of fighting and the cries of the

wounded and dying.

"Here we go again!" she said to the others, her eyebrows raised in the acceptence that another adventure awaited them on the turn of a handle.

Sam opened the door and peered within.

Lancelot rose groggily, every muscle aching as if he'd been running for hours. He instinctively glanced at Guinevere and in the flickering light of the dying fire, he could just make out the subtle rise and fall of her chest. 'She is still alive! 'he thought, 'but for how long can she survive in this comatose state?'

Some instinct had woken him, his senses, despite being weaker since arriving here, alert enough to know that something was amiss. Instinct also made him reach for his sword and rise quietly, while listening out for any sound that should not be there. The night was just turning to day as the sun rose above the horizon, casting a thin beam of light through the narrow rock entrance. 'Surely they have not found us already, 'he thought, his mind racing.

A shadow passed across the opening, bringing him fully alert now to the possible dangers. A loud metronomic whomping sound gradually got louder and louder. 'Dragon!' he thought, wide eyed and alert. 'I must protect Guinevere,' he thought as he looked behind him, seeing a spear resting against the wall.

He came out of the opening like a ghost. Nine Skree were just entering the outer cavern, when Lancelot appeared out of the shadows, sword in one hand, spear in the other. The nearest two Skree went down before knowing he was there. The remaining seven backed away quickly, encircling him. Before they could even form a plan, Lancelot strode forward and engaged the one facing him. Out of the corner of his eye, he kept his senses honed on any movement from the others. His normal fast reflexes were diminished, he was fighting at their speed now. Normally, taking out this many Skree would have been easy for him but now with his senses dulled, his stamina running low and his aching limbs, this was a different matter entirely. This was a deadly game where the stakes were high, and the consequences even worse. 'Must protect Guinevere', he thought as he ducked beneath one swing, parried with his sword and drove the spear in deep. Even as the Skree crumpled to the floor dead, two more came at him from both sides. He ducked, back tracked and took them both out as they clattered into each other. Out of the corner of his eye, he saw a larger form wrenching the camouflaged shrubs away to bring in extra light. An Erlking, with bow in one hand, threw the bushes away and entered the melee. Behind him, he saw the gigantic face of a Dragon, it's huge snout snorting smoke as its wings seemed to beat in sync with his own bearing heart. 'Must protect Guinevere,' he thought again as he parried a blow from the Skree on his left while keeping another at arm's length with the point of his spear. An arrow whistled loudly in the cavern thudding into his shoulder, knocking him backwards towards the entrance to the inner cavern. Another struck a Skree who appeared in front of him, talons raised. He heard the Erlking curse and saw him load another arrow. He bounced off the back wall, roared and swung his sword in a deadly arc at the advancing Skree, who didn't even have time to move out of the way. At the same time, he twisted the spear in his right wrist, took his arm back and released it with tremendous force, even as the Erlking fired. The arrow and the spear missed each other by a fraction of an inch as they both travelled on their deadly paths. The Erlking dropped to his knees, the spear embedded in his chest even as the second arrow struck Lancelot in his chest. The impact pushed him back on unsteady legs, as he looked down in amazement at the two arrows that protruded from him. A Skree came in for the kill but even as his eyes started to water, so Lancelot had the presence of mind to duck, move to his left and dispatch the advancing Skree in its tracks.

As if in slow motion, he saw the Dragon roar and set itself to release its fiery breath upon the cavern. Everything, even Guinevere would perish if it released its fiery salvo. He looked to his right and saw the remaining Skree pushing its way through the opening to get at Guinevere. To his left, the Dragon took in a deep breath and opened its mouth, its large sharp stained teeth gleaming in the early morning light. He saw the Erlking slumped to the floor, its eyes frosted over in the embrace of death, the spear, the Dragon slayer spear, still protruding from its chest. With great effort, he stumbled forward reached the Erlking and pulled the spear out. At the back of the Dragon's throat he saw the tiny spark of a flame within the darkness, and he knew he was moments away from being consumed in fire. He could hear the Dragon's wings again, the rhythm of its beating almost hypnotic in its whomping up and down, up and down, as the Dragon held its position. In his semi-conscious state, he noticed its grey scales and bony hide, its large reptilian eyes, the yellow irises peering at him as if he were a mere insect.

Again, he twirled the spear in his hand to get a firm grip and the balance right, then strode forward out of the opening onto the ledge, appearing into the dawn's early light to get within almost touching distance of the huge grey snout. If the Dragon had ever known fear at any time in its life, the moment a bloodied and dying human with a spear in its hand emerging from the darkness of the overhanging rock, then this was the time. Its dark lidless eyes looked on, the corneas narrowing as it noticed and felt the power of the weapon in the Guardian's hand. Its simple brain that knew nothing but how to instill fear to all before it, bar its lord, suddenly felt a completely new sensation. For once, it was the hunted. Its mind seemed to compute, too late, that not all Humans were weak, some had a back bone and the will to fight back. Lancelot released the spear from almost point-blank range and without even looking, turned and threw his sword with the other hand. The spear entered the opened mouth of the Dragon, flying past its teeth to drive deep into its throat. The fire bolt never appeared. The dragon screamed, a bellow so loud, the air itself shook. The creature lost its balance in mid-air as the wings ceased to flap and it crashed forward into the ledge, as its eyes started to glaze over in shock. It's huge bulk, no longer held in the air by its powerful wings, plummeted downwards. Lancelot sank to his knees watching as his sword cartwheeled through the air and struck the last remaining Skree in the back, killing it instantly, wedging it between the narrow opening.

The Dragon tried to flap its wings once to stay upright but failed and dropped like a stone to crash onto the rocks below with a reverberating whump, before lying still, its eyes staring into nothing, dead.

Lancelot fell backwards, his lifeblood mixing with those who he had hunted nearly his whole life. He tried to rise but found he couldn't. All was silent now, bar the crashing waves below as the land and the sea fought their eternal daily battle for control. Even as his eyes glazed over, his thoughts were of Guinevere and the three young Guardians. 'Please succeed, my friends,' he thought, 'Don't let me die in vain,' he closed his eyes for the final time. 'At least, Guinevere is safe,' and he smiled his last.

CHAPTER 6 - AVALON

Sam swung the door open and saw a line of four stairs leading upwards. Someone ran past the opening and they all flinched. The noise was almost deafening now. It seemed that they had entered into the very centre of the battle. She remembered Gawain's conversation with Arthur about how fierce the fighting was. She turned back to the others who were huddled on the stairs.
"Shadowchasers," she whispered.
"Good idea," Chloe nodded.
"We are meant to be trying to find this Tristan guy without being seen," Jazz reminded them.
Sam looked at Chloe and lowered her eyes.
"Staffs at the ready then," she quipped, grasping it in both hands.
It was then that they heard the sound of a horn and the almost immediate cessation of the fighting. A deathly silence held sway for a few moments, the only sound to break it was coming from the cries of the wounded and dying. Smoke drifted across the entrance and they glimpsed ghostly figures moving within.
Sam took the plunge and walked up the stairs to enter a stone building that was made up of one huge long room with arched windows along both sides and a set of massive doors in front of them at the other end of the room. Behind them on a large circular raised plinth, a Hag Stone rested, and Sam glimpsed a group of people huddled together, nearby. People were everywhere. At least twenty or so Knights and warriors were guarding the double doors. Huge wooden beams were strung across the doors as extra support. The six windows on each side were shuttered and had slits in them for arrows to be fired. Some were smoking and burning, causing wisps of smoke to swirl in the air within the building. Every window was guarded by two warriors, one with a bow and one with a spear. Above their heads, arched wooden rafters supported a roof that was enshrouded in darkness. Bodies lay every-

where, the intensity of the battle giving no one the chance to tend to the dead. A row of people, the wounded who could no longer help, sat only a few yards from them, their backs against the stone wall, some moaning with the pain of their injuries, their eyes glazed over in shock. People were choking from the smoke which billowed around the room as if looking for a way to escape. Sam sensed a light appear behind her and they all turned to see one of the most beautiful sights they had ever seen.

The hole within the Hag Stone hole suddenly lit up, casting an eerie glow around the plinth and the surrounding area, bathing those standing close to it in a bright light that made them raise their hands to their faces to shield themselves. The hole shimmered and then took form showing a picture of a causeway and in the distance, the gleaming spires of a city.

'I've seen that place before! ' she thought in amazement. 'When Merlin showed me his vision, that was the city I glimpsed along the stone causeway.'

"It's a 'Stargate'!" Chloe exclaimed, her mouth dropping open in awe.

The scene showed a stone bridge leading off across a sea, or river, towards a distant spired city, that glimmered in the sun. The cobbled causeway was empty apart from one figure that seemed to step into the picture and through it, Guinevere! The three girls turned away, concealing themselves and covering their faces as best they could. They all knew she should not see them here.

"Gawain, head back to Arthur and tell him what is happening here. I can only keep this open for a short while, but it should be enough time to get everyone through. I'll send Merlin back to seal this, and the cavern entrance. We can't hold out any longer. There is no time to waste, the tree is safe, I'll take the Books back next, tell him that."

"Yes, my lady." Gawain replied.

The girls huddled closer together as a figure approached and went past them down the stairs.

"Tristan, get the wounded, women and children through first, hurry," she said with a voice of authority that they had not heard

from her before. "Tell the Knights to hold on until everyone is through ..." she left the last sentence unfinished. "I'll send Merlin back to destroy this Hag Stone, it is the only way we can be safe."
"Yes, my lady," a young voice replied. There was a pause.
"Yes, Tristan?"
"And you, my lady, shouldn't you be going back through?"
"My place is with my people, I will not leave them until they are all safe on Avalon. We shall leave no one behind. The Books will stay close to me until we get them to Avalon. Now, get these people through as quick as you can and lead them to Avalon, then return and I'll send more through."
Sam looked at Jazz, eyebrows raised, eyes wide.
"Now's the time," Sam said to them.
"I agree," whispered a voice from her shoulder.
Jazz and Chloe nodded, and they all stepped out from the stone staircase and up onto the plinth, to join the other people waiting beside the Hag Stone. The light was almost blinding, so bright was the view coming from the hole in the Stone. They huddled together with six others, barely a yard from Guinevere, their heads turned away. Three women, one elderly man and two teenage children stood in the group, looking dishevelled and exhausted. All wore brown monk-like robes that were held in place by a belt of rope, tied twice around their waists. Whether they were monks or worked at a monastery, they could not tell, but they all stood there in silence, shock etched across their faces.
'Of course, we are at the Abbey,' Sam thought.
She braved a glance towards a young man who was approaching them, this could only be Tristan. The young man was tall and thin, and walked with a gangly lope. His dishevelled black hair hung upon a lean angular face that was all sharp edges. His brown eyes were light and warm, and a line of freckles dotted across his face and forehead. The first growth of a beard was beginning to poke through, giving him a more masculine look than his slim frame denoted. He wore boots and tanned breeches, with a white stained shirt and a black leather waistcoat. A scabbard was tied around his waist and a long sword was held in his right hand, the

tip showing crimson splotches that showed he had already faced some action that day.

Sam looked at his features again, some familiarity crossing her already tired mind. Some inner sense said that she had already met this boy before but that was impossible, she knew. Yet a strange feeling of déjà vu attached itself to her thoughts. 'I know this young man, I have met him somewhere before. But where?' Tristan stood facing them, a puzzled expression on his face when he spotted the three of them huddled behind the monks.

"This way, please, we must hurry, you will be safe through here, I promise," he said with a smile. His voice was strong and authoritative for one so young, and it was one Sam had definitely heard before. Yet then it had been a voice of a man, not a boy, but the tone was the same, the way he spoke, it was unmistakable, Lorofax!

With her mind in turmoil, she waited in line as one by one, the wounded and the monks stepped through the hole in the Stone, and down some steps in the bottom of the picture, to appear on the causeway. It was an incredible sight to see. It was like watching a magic show on TV, she thought, but this was real which made it all the more amazing. They had already passed through many Hag Stones on their journeys, but not one like this that was set open by Guinevere's magic.

Suddenly behind them a huge boom echoed through the room, as something huge struck the doors from outside. The timbers and door groaned but held fast. Dust dropped to the ground from the rafters and the whole building seemed to shake. Everything seemed to happen at once. A large piece of the ceiling suddenly dropped to the floor with a massive crash. Stone and rubble peppered the people closest to it, knocking some to the floor. A billowing dust cloud swept around the room, making it almost impossible to see. Sam glimpsed up to see daylight though the opening that was suddenly blocked out by a huge two headed figure, out of everyone's worst nightmare. A giant three fingered hand reached down and through. Knights ran forward to stab and prod at the thing with swords and spears. In one quick motion, the hand squatted a hapless Knight into the air to be dashed against a wall, where he slumped to the ground in a heap and lay still. More warriors thrust spears at the hand and a voice bellowed from outside in pain before the giant quickly withdrew the hand out of the hole.

The opening shimmered for an instant as Guinevere sagged to the floor momentarily, her concentration lost. And then, the image cleared and was solid again.

"This way, hurry," Tristan was saying, as Sam looked back towards Guinevere. For the briefest of moments, their eyes met and to Sam's utter amazement, Guinevere smiled at her and nodded. The door shuddered again with another resounding boom and the sound of splintered wood was followed by a hushed silence from everyone within. Some Knights put their weight against the door as another boom shattered the timbers, and smashed the door into pieces, scattering the Knights like skittles in a game of tenpin bowling. A seething mass of Skree and Erlking started to force their way through the gaps. Knights and warriors rushed forward and engaged the enemy, holding them back with their sheer will to survive and protect their people. The fighting was fierce and brutal with no quarter given or expected.

By now, all the monks had gone through and Tristan was urging them forward.

"We have to help!" Chloe said, her voice breaking.

"We have to stick to our task, Chloe," Jazz said, holding her in both hands, her staff resting against her shoulder. "We need to speak to him," she said nodding her head towards the Squire. "Nothing else matters, even this. Please, Chloe."

Suddenly a horde of Skree broke through, and fighting erupted all over the room. In moments the place was going to be lost, this was the last stand. Guinevere rose and backpedalled to the Stone, her eyes wide. Only a few warriors standing between her and a group of advancing Skree. A group of Knights hacked their way towards the pedestal and surrounded it, protecting Guinevere. The rest were bundled through the opening one after the other as quickly as they could go. Chloe raced to some recently injured

warriors and lifted the closest one, helping him up the pedestal and into the hole. Sam and Jazz seeing this, quickly followed suit. The intense fighting was barely yards from them now, and only a few remained in the room. The three of them, eight Knights, Guinevere and Tristan.
"My lady," Tristan shouted.
"Help these three through, Tristan and I will follow, I promise," she said pushing three men forward that had appeared out of the gloom. She turned and spoke to the nearest Knight, who looked over his shoulder quizzically at his Queen. 'What is she doing?' Sam thought.
The Knight bent and retrieved a small ornately carved box, and slung it over his back and fastened it there with some rope that was tied through two holes on either end of the box. He stepped close to Guinevere and backtracked with the group up on to the pedestal.
'The Books.' Sam thought.
The Knight raised his eyes to Guinevere, a look of calm determination and pride on his young bloodied face. Behind them the room had filled with Skree and Erlking. The Knights as if they had trained for this, hacked, parried and stabbed at the seething mass in front of them, while at the same time retreating step by step towards the opening. Just before the three girls were bundled through, Sam looked to her right and realised that the Knight closest to her was actually Merlin. He was standing a little behind the group, his eyes half shut, as if in meditation. He seemed almost oblivious to the rearguard action, and seemed to be focussing on something else. A faint rumbling rose over the sound of the fighting. A few Erlking straightened and looked around as if sensing something. The Skree, seemingly oblivious, came on in relentless waves. One broke through and was brought down by the blade of the Knight holding the box. The rumbling increased. Sam, Chloe and Jazz stepped through and looked back as the walls of the building started to collapse. Guinevere stepped through, followed by the Knights leaving only Merlin alone with his back to them; half in, half out of the hole in the Stone. The roof came

down with a massive crash as the supports holding it up toppled and caved in, burying the hapless Erlking and Skree beneath tons of rubble and wood. A dust cloud erupted out of the opening covering the retreating party in a film of grey soot. Merlin stepped backwards and the scene disappeared.
'It is done," he said solemnly to Guinevere.
They stood huddled close together on the stone staircase that led down to the causeway.
Guinevere looked shocked and upset, the loss of life weighing heavy in her mind. "It had to be done," she replied after a pause. "Merlin, head back through, get a message to the King and if it looks like the outcome is dire, destroy that Stone, at all costs! Don't let Moribund use it, he could march his whole army on Avalon."
"Yes, my lady."
Sam looked at the bedraggled group. Instinctively, she looked out of the corner of her eye for Thorfell. She was so used to him being there now, that she couldn't sense if he was there. "I'm still here," he whispered to her and sheltered himself out of sight. "Could do with a rest though."
"I'm the one doing the walking," she whispered back.
"I know, but it's been a tiring day just hanging on, you know." Sam let out a small chuckle. "Glad you're still with us, Thorfell."
"Believe me, so am I!"
Sam turned her attention back to the remaining Knights. All were covered in dust, from head to foot. Blood seeping from their wounds stood out against the dust covered features, yet not one complained. Everyone looked exhausted but determined to carry on. Now that they were through, the sight that beheld them was incredible. The stone causeway was at least twenty yards wide, and seemed to stretch in both directions for as far as they could see. To their right, it disappeared into a shimmering mirage, as if it went on forever. To their left, the glimmering spires of a city could be seen, upon an island that looked bright and verdant in contrast to the colour of the sea. It was hard to fathom how far away it was due to the mirage effect. A sea, so blue in

colour it almost looked unreal, stretched on either side of them to distant horizons. They were at least forty feet above the sea, which was almost calm, and Sam could glimpse movement beneath the waves. A pod of dolphins bobbed up and dived under, all in the blink of an eye. Up they came again as if riding some underwater carnival wheel, before disappearing under the bridge and out of sight. The bridge floor was cobbled and on each side a low wall ran along its length. At regular intervals, a series of arches stretched up and over the bridge. On each of these, Sam could see a line of stone stairs, leading up to what looked like more Hag Stones. The sun was out, the light almost blinding at first until they acclimatised. Everything seemed so bright and clear compared to the darkness of their previous location. 'It felt like a different day, a different time,' she thought.

It had taken less than half an hour to reach the island, when it had seemed like it would take all day. After passing under the first arch, the island had suddenly appeared much closer. After passing under the second arch, the island now stood before them in all its beauty and grandeur.
The island rose out of the sea, as if it had been pushed up from the sea floor. Sandy beaches encircled its base, leading to a dense green jungle. The land gradually rose towards a walled city, beyond. A series of giant waterfalls cascaded down to a river that cut through the jungle like a knife, its waters fast flowing and eager to reach the sea. The causeway carried on over the land, and on towards the city. Sam couldn't see if the bridge continued beyond the city, but somehow she felt that it did not.
"*All roads lead to Avalon,*" Tristan had told them.
"You mean, a*ll roads lead to Rome,*" Chloe had replied.
Tristan had laughed, and Sam had seen Chloe blush slightly at this. "That saying was copied by the Romans," he had said with a wink and a smile towards Chloe.
They had caught up with Tristan and fallen in beside him, almost

as soon as they had reached the bridge. The group of stragglers were spread out along the causeway. The wounded were being helped along by the Knights. Their shields were on their backs and swords sheathed, sensing that there was no longer any danger. Guinevere was walking ahead of them with the Knight with the box and one other, deep in conversation. When they had fallen in step with Tristan, he had peered their way and frowned.

"I have not seen you before? Are you from the Abbey?"

"Not quite," Chloe replied.

"We are here to seek your help," Jazz said, getting straight to the point.

"Mine," he replied, looking briefly towards Guinevere and the Knights. "I am but a Squire, what would you want of me that you can't ask for from the Knights?"

"Lancelot sent us," Jazz said.

Tristan stopped walking and looked from one to the other, his face a mask of questions and suspicion. "If this is one of his stupid tricks, now is not the time," he said and started off again.

Jazz raised her eyebrows and shook her head. "He said you might not believe us, he said to say that *time is a law that has no respect for who you are.*"

The young Squire paused again and turned to them. "He said for you to say that, really, that's amazing, I never thought he listened to a single word I uttered, I am amazed. Very well, you have my attention. Come walk with me and ask of me what you wish."

After a few minute's conversation, he stopped again and looked at them, his eyes wide. "What, you want me to break in to the Hall of Artefacts and steal the Spear of Destiny?"

"That's a cool name," Chloe said.

"Which one, the Hall of Artefacts or the Spear of Destiny?" Jazz said sarcastically.

"Both, actually," Chloe replied unperturbed.

The conversation had slowed their pace, so much so, that by now, the group had fallen behind the main group by quite some distance. Only the three that had been helped through together were anywhere near them now, they huddled together shuffling along at a steady pace, a few hundred feet ahead of them.

"Lancelot needs that Spear to stop Moribund when he comes in through the battlements at Tor Burr."

"And you know this, how?" he questioned.

The girls looked at each other, not knowing how to explain without giving too much away.

"Never mind," he said, interrupting their thoughts. "If Lancelot needs that Spear then so be it, we will have to retrieve it." Sam could see his mind mulling over things and a nerve under his right eye twitched, making her think that he wasn't fully comfortable with what he was about to do. "But we will need a distraction," he added.

They were above the island now, the causeway winding gradually up and towards the city. Below them, they passed a range of cliffs where a waterfall toppled off the edge to cascade into a lagoon that was surrounded by palms and a small tributary that meandered down to a beach. The water frothed and churned where it hit the lagoon, but soon cleared a short way out to create a tranquil picture of unspoiled beauty, the water blue and clear. A road had been carved out of the rock zigzagging from the top to the bottom, and they glimpsed figures on horseback riding up its steep incline. Other figures could be seen walking up and down carrying things.

The tops of buildings appeared as they crested a small rise and they stopped dead in their tracks in awe and looked down upon a city of unimaginable beauty and splendour. To the girls, the structures looked like they had gone back in time to ancient Greece. A huge Acropolis sat at the centre of the city, its marble columns glinting in the sun. The single detached buildings that were set apart from each other on the rolling hillside resembled Roman villas. Palm, Orange, Lemon and Date trees lined the causeway making Sam suddenly realise that they were no longer on a bridge but on a road leading towards the very heart of the city. The bridge had seamlessly ended and the road continued on. Giant spired towers were set alongside the causeway, some with high walls around them while some sat before an open square, where people were going about their everyday lives. The spires glistened and on closer inspection, they spotted different jewels and stones imbedded into the roofs of the spires, so that they gleamed in the sun like twinkling stars. Most of the inhabitants wore clothes of white linen or cloth with different coloured rope ties around their waist. Their features were tanned and they looked towards the groups with hardly a backward stare, as if this was just a normal occurrence. In the outskirts, houses were huddled closer together and the streets between the buildings were narrow and teeming with people. Interspersed between the buildings were squares, where markets were taking place. Local citizens moved amongst the stalls bartering and buying produce.

"Welcome to *The isle of Avalon*," Tristan said, "It's beautiful, isn't it?"

"It's amazing," Chloe replied quietly, shaking her head as if she couldn't believe what she was seeing.

"Where's the Hall of Artefacts?" Jazz asked, bringing everyone back to reality.

"It's over there, at the edge of the Acropolis," he said pointing to a tall rectangular building that had a flight of mighty steps leading up to it. "But it will be guarded. Despite the safety here, there are too many powerful artefacts for it to be left unguarded. Some of them also have the power to entrap the weak of mind. It is guarded from noon to night. I don't envy going in there alone," he added. "but I will, if my Charge orders it, I must obey,"

" 24/7," Chloe said.

Tristan looked at Chloe, and frowned.

"It's short for all day," she added with a wink.

He looked at her with quizzical fascination as if she was speaking a different language.

"Never mind," Chloe replied, playfully nudging him with her shoulder.

Sam couldn't believe what she was seeing. Chloe was flirting! Up until now, Chloe had not been interested in boys at all. Yet now, here she was flirting with Tristan, and he in turn was reciprocating. 'Great! 'she thought with a smile, 'that's all we need,' She could see Chloe's cheeks redden a little.

A few moments later, they were standing beside a low wall amongst a crowd of people in the square in front of the Hall of Artefacts. A single Knight sat on an ornate stool at the entrance, idly looking about and looking somewhat bored at his guard duty posting. The square floor was cobbled like all the roads, but in the centre was a giant mosaic, so huge that it must have taken years to build. The picture itself was hard to see as everyone was moving on top of it, but the coloured tiles were depicting some sort of picture of a city and a great battle.

"Leave this to me," Tristan said with more confidence than he felt, "I know the guard," he added.

He was halfway up the steps, when the guard spotted him and rose to his feet, his spear, casually lifting into a position of defence. The Knight was huge, at least six and a half foot tall. He was like a body builder, bulging muscles rippling between his tight outfit. His bearded face and deep-set green eyes, above a squat nose and tight lips, peered down the stairs towards the group, a frown forming lines upon his forehead. The spear in his hand looked like a wand. His eyes widened when he realised it was Tristan and he was about to speak, when a commotion in the square turned his gaze away from them.

Someone screamed, a scream of absolute fear. Someone else screamed and the seed of fear was sown. The crowd in the square, like panicked animals, started to run away from whatever was happening. People were pushed aside, knocked to the floor, bundled over without a second thought. Sam watched as a basket of fruit was knocked out of a woman's hand to scatter Apples and Oranges on the ground. To get out of the way of the oncoming rush, the girls climbed a few of the large steps and looked down on the scene. The square was clearing in moments, with lots of people climbing the steps, obscuring the girls view of what was happening.

Guinevere stood in the centre of the square facing three figures that were changing forms. The Knight with the box on his back stood in front of Guinevere, his sword out. The nearest form flowed like liquid, then reformed into a tall thin man that was cloaked in a dark flowing shiny looking cloth, his features hidden in the shadows beneath a black cape. Two figures behind him were reforming into DemonSkree. With a scream, they charged at the Knight. A body lay on the floor, a dagger in its back, blood forming in pools in the gaps of the mosaics. The Knight was holding his own but the box on his back was hindering his movements. Suddenly the cloaked figure lifted his arm and the solid black shaft of a spear extended from his hand, to strike Guinevere in the chest. The Knight with the box shouted something, dropped his guard and was pounced upon by the two DemonSkree. In the melee, the box was knocked off the Knight's back where it clattered to the floor, bounced twice upon the cobbles and fell at the man's feet. The box lid dropped open revealing the Books of Time. Beneath the cape, the man smiled, reached down and grasped the Books in both hands. The girls saw only glimpses of this as the people shuffled past them and out of harm's way, racing up the steps without any thought apart from to get as far away from the scene as possible.

Out of the corner her eye, Sam saw the guard jump down the steps and fling his spear, as Guinevere fell to the floor, her face a mask of pain. The spear struck one DemonSkree in the chest, then continued on to impale the second in the shoulder, knocking them both off the fallen Knight, onto the cobbles in a bundle of arms and legs, unmoving.

He reached Guinevere and caught her, lowering her to the floor gently, before turning and drawing his sword all in one flowing movement.

"Guinevere!" Sam shouted, suddenly seeing her prone figure and bloodied chest, tears forming in her eyes, through the throng of citizens in front of her.

"Tristan, you have your distraction," Jazz said.

Tristan seemed torn between helping the Knight or carrying out the duty of his charge. He stood transfixed, swaying back and forth, one part of his body seeming to go up while the other part pulling him down towards helping the Knight.

The Knight turned his head, peered at Tristan and called his name, beckoning him to help, while at the same time moving towards the man holding the Books of Time. The young Squire looked Jazz in the eye, shook his head once, anguish written across his young features, then raced up the last few steps and into the Hall of Artefacts. The Knight skidded to a halt in front of the hooded figure, his sandals scraping acoss the stone.
The three girls raced across the steps, and in front of the crowd, to see the guard engage with the hooded man. A shaft of black, shot out from the man's cloaked arm. The guard ducked, parried then brought his sword down on the black tentacle like spear, shattering it into a thousand shards. The man screamed, retracted what was left then turned and fled. The three girls raced across the long steps and got in front of the crowd, just as the figure disappeared down the alley. Sam turned to see Tristan appear and raise something in his hand. Without stopping he leapt down the stairs two at a time.
"I've got it," Tristan said slightly out of breath holding something long in a bundle of cloth. "Come on, no time to lose."
"But Guinevere," Sam said pleading, "She's been struck, she might be dying!" she added, standing her ground as the rest carried on racing down the steps onto the cobbled square.
"Tristan," the guard shouted, urging him to join him.
"Sam, we have to move, we can't help anyone if we stay here. We are signing everyone's death warrants if we don't succeed … you know that," she added more quietly.
Sam shut her eyes briefly as if to blank out the scene, then turned and raced after the other three. "Hold on Thorfell."
"I already am," he squeaked.
"LORAFAX!" the guard shouted again, as he bent over the fallen Knight, before moving on to Guinevere, no one heard him over the noise of their escape. The hooded figure had disappeared into an alley.
Guinevere opened her eyes and looked at the Knight. "George," she said gripping his forearm, straining to speak. "Stop that man, don't let him get away…" Her eyes closed and she slumped onto

the ground, unconscious. George turned and rose like a coiled snake and raced after the hooded man, a grim look of determination etched upon his face.

The four reached the bridge in minutes with no sign of pursuit, and slowed to a brisk walk amongst the throngs going to and fro. Within a few minutes they reached the first arch, and stood before a Hag Stone carved into it. A path had been cut out of the rock around the Stone and the three started to race around it, but were stopped by Tristan's outstretched hand.

"You don't need to do that on the Bridge of Travel, I just need to open it with the correct calling," he added quietly with little conviction.

Tristan stood before the Stone and stared at it a little perplexed. Behind them, they heard the rumble of hooves and saw six Knights upon horseback racing towards them.

The seconds passed as Tristan remained motionless, deep in thought.

"Er, hello, Earth to Tristan," Jazz said exasperated, her nerves frayed. "Anytime today."

"You do know how to use these things?" Sam asked quietly.

"Yes, yes it's just I've forgotten the correct calling for this one. I've only just finished my studies on this, and I can't remember all the callings off by heart yet. I am only a Squire you know."

"Oh, jeez!" Jazz exclaimed. "We are doomed," her normal unruffled thoughts, shattered to the winds.

"Thorfell, can you do anything?"

"I only know a few, and all of them won't lead us to where we want to go."

"Anywhere is better than here!" Jazz added, her voice rising to a high pitch.

"Where did he come from?" Tristan said pointing at the little Pixie in astonishment. "It's a ... it's a ..."

"I'm a Pixie, now concentrate please, young man, a lot depends on this."

"Lancelot entrusted our mission with you, he has faith in you," Chloe said, stepping closer to him, their eyes meeting.

By now, the horsemen were nearly upon them, the noise of the hooves upon the cobbles deafeningly loud.
Chloe's words seemed to have a calming influence on him. He took a deep breath, let it out, then returned his stare to the hole in the Stone. A second later, his face took on a smile of recognition.
"Stop, in the name of Arthur, I demand you to stop," the leading Knight said springing from his horse, which skidded to a halt with a neigh of disapproval. The Knight raced forwards, sword drawn.
Tristan spoke a few words, turned to them and said "Time to go," as he pushed Chloe through, Sam followed with Jazz close behind. The Knight raced up the steps, his armour slowing him down, and was just in time to see Tristan disappear and the hole reset to show the inner wall of the arch again. The knight cursed and swung his sword in annoyance at the stone, making sparks fly as metal struck rock.

CHAPTER 7 - DESOLATION

"It's done," Tristan said, racing back down the stairs to join them beside the Hag Stone, the same Hag Stone that the Guardians and Thorfell knew would soon be destroyed.
"We need to get out of here now, before …," Jazz said whispering. The clang of fighting could be heard above them, and every moment they remained was more time for them to be caught. "before we are seen," she finished.
"But won't we need to wait until Lancelot kills Moribund before we try to go through?" Sam asked.
"Good point. Jazz," Chloe added looking at Jazz for a reply. "No pun intended!" she added with a raise of her eyebrows.
"How the hell should I know," Jazz replied exasperated. "We need to go, now!"
"I believe that if the act is carried out successfully, then it should not matter whether you go before or after it happens, just as long as it happens," Thorfell said from on Sam's shoulder. Tristan was still staring at him, wide eyed.
"You mean we are going home now, home," Chloe said with relief.
"You know, that's the best thing you've ever said, since I met you, Thorfell," Jazz said with a forced smile.
"I have to come with you, I know you are not from this time," Tristan said solemnly. "There is no place for me here, not yet, maybe never," he said, his head bowed with the realisation of what he had done.
"What! You can't come with us, to our time, it wouldn't be right." Jazz said, realising she was owning up to coming from the future.
"Jazz, look at what he has just done, and what he has done for us, we couldn't have done it without him. We owe him and if we can repay him in some way by taking him with us, then that is the least we can do." Sam said, her mind dwelling on the fact that this young man was destined to end up living in a future they were

planning on destroying.

Jazz pinched her lips together, her eyes wide, her normal calm demeanour gone for the time being. "Yes OK, I understand we owe Tristan a lot," she said, coming to a realisation in her mind. "Let's go."

They circled the Stone three times, Chloe dragging Tristan with them and telling him not to look back. They heard footsteps coming down the stairs even as they stepped through the hole and disappeared.

As Arthur crashed into the table by the force of the arrow, in the shadows behind him, Lancelot lifted the spear and twisted it in his grip, to feel its balance. 'This was one strange day,' he thought, 'even for a Guardian!' He had already inspected the spear. Its polished wooden shaft was knotted and aged but smooth to the touch. Gold metal bands, about two inches deep were wrapped around the wood at regular intervals. On the bands, intricate carvings and writings showed scenes and language from a bygone time. The point was cast in iron, polished to a shine and tipped with a clear stone that shone with a luminous blue glow. Where he held it, he could feel the faint impression in the wood where it had worn down from the warriors who had held it through the mists of time. He almost sensed someone else's presence around him as he raised the spear above his shoulder. This was the fabled spear that should be in the Hall of Antiquities on Avalon, yet here it was, placed here by the hands of his Squire with a cryptic answer of how he had acquired it, and why he should be using it now. In all his life as a Guardian, he had seen many strange things, but this one, this strange mystery, was one that he didn't know how to unravel.

All this went through his mind, in a brief moment, as he launched himself out of the shadows to protect his King. A King, his friend, who in the heat of the battle, had called him a coward. With the red mist flowing, Arthur had accused him of the worst thing a

Knight could hear, cowardice. That stung more than he thought, but he knew he was no coward and Arthur knew it as well. It had actually been the fear of the King himself, of losing this battle, that had made Arthur lash out at the nearest one to him, and that had been Lancelot. Anyway, he was a Knight of the Round Table and Arthur was his King, so no matter what Arthur thought, he was going to protect him to his dying breath.

Even as Moribund appeared through the smashed door and stood framed against the light, he knew why he was holding this spear, he knew why Tristan had put it there. This spear was a Dragon slayer and bringer of righteousness, all rolled into one. Now was the time to put an end to this, to stop Moribund and end this war, to bring forth the Second Age of Man.

"Monster," he heard Arthur say.

"Take him," Moribund said to the Skree standing next to the evil magician.

From the shadows Lancelot threw the spear with all his might, it flew true and straight striking Moribund square in the chest, knocking him back into an Erlking, bowling them both over.

He jumped from the table and skidded to a halt beside a startled and bloodied King. Their eyes locked, Arthur's dropping first. Lancelot stepped in front of his King, and shielded him from the onslaught. His sword sang a bloody song of death with every swipe and thrust. He knew though, even as he had leapt forward to protect Arthur, that there were just too many and it would be over in moments. Arthur knew it too but he pushed himself up off the table and strode forward to join Lancelot.

It was then that three large spiderlike creatures with semi-human looking bodies shot past the two and attacked the Skree, pushing them back with the ferocity of their attack. Arthur looked at Lancelot with disbelief and with renewed hope. Together with the spider creatures, they forced the Skree back and out of the broken gate, leaving a bloodied trail of dead Skree in their wake. The three creatures forced the last Skree out, and stood like silent sentinels protecting the shattered entrance.

"My God, that was fun, Lancelot," Arthur said with a grimace of pain.

"We need to go now, while we can," Lancelot said, lifting Arthur and walking him towards the stairs. He saw the three Guardians, peering over the top. "Thank you," he said to them as he shuffled passed them and started down the stairs, "I need to get him to safety."

It wasn't long after the battle had finished that Lancelot stepped into the cavern beneath Tor Burr. He'd left Arthur with Merlin and Gawain and had given them orders of what to do. The Giants of Cornwall had arrived to help turn the tide. Moribund was dead, his army would soon be banished back beneath the Earth. All Lancelot had to do was retrieve the spear and take it back to Avalon. He longed to see Guinevere and returning the spear was a good excuse, not that he needed one. He fought for her, their unborn children and their future freedom.

The place still smelt of sweat and death to him. Fear still hung heavy in the air. Only the silence denoted that the fighting was over, the dead were dead, the living glad to be alive. He was not alone. People were starting to clear up the desolation. Funeral pyres would soon litter the landscape. The price of freedom always came at a cost. No war had casualties on just one side. He looked at the fallen, ashen faced and locked in the rigor of death, their features sometimes serene, while others wore a grimace of fear, anguish and pain. One of them could easily have been him, he thought. He strode forward past some Knights, who nodded to him and stood upon the last parapet that was standing, looking down on a scene of utter desolation. Bodies lay everywhere. He shook his head, 'so much death,' he thought. 'Behold, I am death, the bringer of light and disciple of change.' he thought, remembering the line from one of the ancient texts in the library on Avalon. 'And I am that disciple of change, a true bringer of death.'

A cool wind ruffled his long and tousled, black hair and he took a few deep breaths, feeling good to be alive. His King was alive but in a deep sleep which meant he was now in charge, until the King awakened. He looked about him for the spear and saw it standing upright stuck in a prone figure that was lying on top of another larger form. He realised the spear had passed through Moribund and killed the Erlking behind. He smiled inwardly at his prowess and strode towards the dead figure of Moribund, but as he got closer he realised that something was terribly wrong.

"That isn't Moribund," he said aloud, standing before the body, as fear encroached upon his normal calm mentality. 'It's a Demon-Skree, a shapechanger, which means Moribund is still alive and well, and still a major threat to the safety of this land.' He drew his sword and peered around quickly as if expecting Moribund to appear, but only a few stares from the nearest Knights and warriors met his gaze.

"Sire?" the nearest Knight asked him.

He waved him down with an abrupt swish of his sword before sheathing it again. In both hands he grasped and withdrew the spear from the two corpses and stood looking at it for a moment, before heading back towards the tunnels and onwards to Avalon and Guinevere. 'Where are you Moribund?' he thought worriedly, 'What are you up to?'

Sam came through the hole and entered the cold dark water. Before she could even react, water entered her mouth, just as her head broke the surface and she spluttered and coughed out water while trying to keep afloat. The shock had been mind-numbing. Her senses were reeling. They had come back through the Thurle Stone! How had that happened? They were back in the future when they should be coming out in Lancelot's cavern beneath the moor in their time! What had gone wrong?

"Thorfell!" she screamed over her thrashing, realising too late that he might have slipped off. "I'm here," he said in front of her. He was holding onto her staff which was bobbing up and down in the waves. She glimpsed his tiny form holding on to the wood with both arms wrapped around it. Despite her predicament, she forced a smile and grasped the staff, lifting him up so he could jump onto her head.

"Help, I can't swim," a voice said from a body floundering in the water behind her. Tristan was sinking and flapping his arms, as his armour and heavy clothes dragged him under. She saw Jazz and Chloe turn to help, shock written upon their tired faces. Sam's feet suddenly touched bottom and she straightened up, her torso rising above the waves.

"Tristan," she shouted over his thrashing, moving towards him, "just stand up, it's not that deep." Her voice seemed to get through to him and she could see him straighten his body beneath the water and touch bottom.

"Oh," he said a little ashamedly. "I can't swim," he added.

"Don't they teach you anything at Knights school?" Chloe chuckled splashing him with water, with the flick of her wrist.

"Hey," he said and smiled.

They stood there in the shallow water beneath the Stone, looking about them, shivering.

"I said the correct calling to get us home," Thorfell said, "somehow, it's thrown us back here!"

"Something's gone wrong," Chloe said, shaking uncontrollable, her teeth chattering as she spoke.

"We need to get out of the water, come on," Jazz said, pushing her way towards the rocks.

The day was brighter than most, a fading sun poking through the low clouds to warm the day. The tide was going out, leaving the rocks slippery and covered in fresh seaweed. They looked up towards the Dragons nest and saw no movement. 'They were dead. Weren't they? ' Sam thought. As if in response to her thoughts, they glimpsed a part of a large Dragon carcass stuck on the rocks, barely twenty yards from them. Large segments had been torn from it showing a row of huge teeth marks. 'The sea creature I sensed,' she pondered, suddenly very glad to be out of the water. They reached the beach and huddled together, the warmth of the sun gradually drying their clothes. Tristan withdrew his sword and tipped his scabbard up to empty the water onto the sand.

"We failed," Jazz said quietly. "Moribund succeeded in changing time, that's why we can't get home."

"Where are we?" Tristan asked.

"We are in the future. A future rewritten by Moribund where all Humans are slaves," replied Jazz.

'And where your future self is in the forest close to us, 'Sam thought in panic.

"How? We did everything right. Perhaps Lancelot missed or didn't kill Moribund," Jazz said.

"Lancelot does not miss," Tristan replied quickly, "ever."

"He's like Legolas, from *The Lord of the Rings*, then," Chloe said smiling at Jazz.

"Legolas?" Tristan asked.

"Chloe," Jazz exclaimed, eyes wide.

"I'll tell you about him one day," she said with a wink to the Squire.

"Then, how has this happened?" said Jazz.

"I don't know. We need to head back to Lancelot and Guinevere, speak to them, explain what happened," Sam replied.

"Yes, but it's a day's hike back and dangerous," Jazz acknowledged.

"Lancelot and Guinevere are here?" Tristan asked. Jazz nodded.

"I don't think I can make it without some food and rest," Sam heard herself saying, "I'm exhausted, we all need some sleep. Do you think the forest is safe?"

It was then that they heard the sound of mewling coming from the cliff top. They looked up as one. It was coming from the Dragons nest, and the sound was one that they had heard before. It was coming from a baby Dragon.

"We have to take it with us, we can't leave it here, it will die." Sam said.

"It's a Dragon!" Jazz said disbelieving.

"It's a baby." Sam said.
"Have you banged your head or something?"
"I think that was you."
" Then I think I haven't woken up yet. We can't take a Dragon with us, even if it is a baby."
"It is very cute." Chloe added with a smile.
"And so are Lion cubs."
"I think it's a good idea," Tristan said.
"And why's that?"
"We can learn from it, even train it to help us."
"We could keep it in the Fairy Realm, safe from Humans." Thorfell said, stroking its head.
"That's if we can get home! And if we don't?"
"Then we have a new companion, an ally to train."
"OK, I give in, take the thing, but for goodness sake, don't name it."
"Here Peggy," Chloe said, kneeling in front of the thing, calling to it.
"Oh, give me strength," Jazz said, raising her eyes to the heavens.
They had walked along the beach and then clambered up onto the scorched area and headed towards the Dragons nest, their wet shoes making marks through the charred area. The Dragons den was a huge bird's nest made of branches, even full trees that seemed to have been uprooted, and other bits of rubbish that had been washed up on the beach. Dried seaweed and shrubs had been interweaved into the nest, forming a mesh that solidified it into a more solid structure. The smell of Sulphur was everywhere. Another smell, one of burnt cooked meat hung in the air. To their left and further inland, they glimpsed a large pile of dung.
"Er, Dragon poo!" Chloe said, turning up her nose in disgust.
Thats when the baby Dragon suddenly appeared, standing on the edge of the nest, mewling at them. They all looked at each other and then back to the baby Dragon.
"It's tiny." Chloe said.
The thing was the size of a cat. Its tiny legs were thick as was the grey leathery hide that covered its body. Its snout was larger in comparison to its body and almost seemed too big for its torso.

A ridge ran down its head to the end of its snout. Tiny ears protruded high up on either side of its head tucked in behind large snake like eyes. Its tail swished back and forth, a tiny point protruding from its end, sticking upwards from the tip.
It's mewling grew louder as they approached, but it wasn't one of fear, but of pleading.
"It's hungry," Thorfell said.
"Great, what do you feed a baby Dragon?" Jazz asked.
"Human probably!" Tristan said clambering up the side of the nest to peer in. "Don't come any further," he uttered suddenly. "I don't think it's hungry, I think it's just missing its parents." His face had gone ashen and he shuffled off the edge to rejoin them.
"Come on, show me the way to Lancelot, we have much to discuss." he said, shepherding them away quickly. "Which way?" he said to Jazz.
Sam's mind was racing. If they go through the forest, the young Tristan Lorofax could meet the old Tristan Lorofax. This could not be allowed to happen. 'I must speak to Lorofax before we enter the woods,' she thought. She took a deep breath, feeling the air expanding her lungs. She shut her eyes, and let out her breath slowly, trying to remember how they communicated. 'Lorofax,' she spoke out in her mind, 'can you hear me?' she paused, waiting for a response. 'Are you there?' Nothing, no buzzing in her head. She somehow sensed an emptiness in the void. 'Is anyone there?' Nothing again, not a sound in response.
"Sam," It was Thorfell who brought her back.
"I was trying to make contact with Lorofax," she said quietly to him.
"I sense that he is gone, I feel nothing, he's not there, I'm sure of it," he said.
"OK, that helps, but where's he gone?"
"He lost his Wasps, he has no protection, he has to move his family on, find a new place, safe away from the Skree hunting parties. I think he has headed deeper into the forest."
"That makes sense."
"Are you two coming or just waiting for more Dragons to show

up?" Chloe asked. She was holding the baby Dragon under one arm, while leaning on the staff looking back at Sam and Thorfell.

Sam nodded her head sideways to bring Chloe back towards them. She trotted over, nodding towards Tristan. "That is the young Lorafax."

Chloe's eyes raised when her mind suddenly realised the situation.

"It's OK, it seems Lorafax has gone. I'll talk to Tristan, you go ahead and tell Jazz."

"On it," Chloe said, turning and racing forward, stopping to ask Tristan to head back to talk to Sam.

"We rested in the forest last time, we need to get there and get some shut eye," Sam said to the approaching Squire.

"Shut eye?"

"Sleep," she answered.

"OK, that makes sense."

"We've also got a river to cross and there is another nest of Dragons further on, that we'll need to keep away from," Behind Tristan, Sam saw Chloe rest her staff against her side, then raise her hand, her thumb up.

"OK, that makes sense." Tristan said again, a frown forming on his face as he saw Sam's eyes looking behind him. He turned his head quizzically, his thoughts his own. He shook his head once. "Then we had better get going then, I'm tired too."

The journey back to the cave was uneventful but still took more than a day. It was early evening when they got to the concealed gorse entrance.

They entered the forest and quickly found where they had settled down before, made themselves comfortable, then decided who would take first watch. Tristan accepted and it wasn't until they all woke up that they realised he had stood watch all night. Sam's stomach rumbled with the lack of food and she couldn't even remember the last time she had eaten something. Later that day they had reached the river and decided to head upstream, around the bend and out of sight of the Dragons nest. Eventually they reached a point where they could safely wade across the river. Heading back down river, they found the path that led to the Lorofax's camp. The destroyed rope bridge hung in tatters to their left, a stark reminder that Dragons were close.

They had reached the giant tree and Lorofax's hideout, and found it deserted. As if he had sixth sense, a table of food and drink lay waiting for them. The girls looked at each other wondering how he had known. They tucked into the food, instantly feeling refreshed and more alive. The place was eerily quiet without the buzzing of the Wasps, and Sam felt a tug of guilt that they had been a big part of what had happened here.

Leaving the forest and heading across the open expanse before reaching the rocks had been the scariest part of the return journey, but they had made it safely. They had retraced their steps, stopping only once when a party of Skree, leading a bedraggled looking bunch of Humans, came over a rise barely twenty yards from them. They sank to the floor, burying themselves behind some burnt tree stumps. The group headed off, the sound of a whip in the hand of the Erlking leader, cracking loud in the silence as they huddled together. The low murmuring of the Humans was audible between the whip cracks. Tristan turned pale at the sight. "My God, I had not realised what it was like until now," he said quietly as the group headed off to the north of them.

Chloe held the baby Dragon close, one hand across its tiny snout. It had fallen asleep for nearly the whole journey back having tucked into some of the food. The group had taken it in turns to carry the baby Dragon, and Sam could swear that it had grown already. It also felt heavier to carry than it looked and Sam was relieved when she handed it to Tristan.

The sun, hidden behind the low cloud was hanging low in the sky by the time they reached the concealed entrance, pulled it back, entered and replaced it.

"Something's wrong," Thorfell said in Sam's ear. She waved for everyone to stop.

"Lancelot would be here to meet us, he would know we were close," Thorfell said, replying to their stares. He looked pensive and more frightened than he had ever looked.

They raced to the cliff edge and looked down. They saw the dead Dragon at the bottom of the cliff. The steps down to the cave were still there and Sam wondered whether they had just come out of the cliff face when they had arrived or had they been left out for some time. They moved down the steps as fast as they could to reach the cave entrance. Tristan led the way, his sword drawn, while Sam brought up the rear. By the time Sam stepped onto the thin ledge before the overhang and entrance to the cave, Tristan was kneeling beside a figure, his body wracked with great sobs.

"It's Lancelot, he's dead!" Jazz said to Sam, tears drawing lines down her dirty cheeks.

"Oh no," her legs gave way as the words sank in. She collapsed and Chloe caught her as they moved closer to the silent figure, and Tristan. Other figures lay close by in the shadows. They counted nine Skree and an Erlking, all dead by Lancelot's hand. Lancelot lay with his back to the wall, his eyes shut, two arrows protruding from his body.

In a daze, Sam saw Jazz clamber over a dead Skree to enter the cave beyond, then return. She felt a roaring in her ears as if she had just stopped after a long run. None of this seemed real. This couldn't be happening. Everything was going wrong. They were trapped here.

Now that the place was secure, Chloe placed the sleeping baby Dragon down beside the inner wall and turned to stare at the silent form of Guinevere, her face full of anguish and loss. 'We have already seen too much death for ones so young,' thought Sam.

"She's in some kind of deep sleep. She's alive, but I can't wake her." she heard Jazz say.

"He died protecting Guinevere," Tristan said quietly. "He killed nine Skree, an Erlking and a Dragon, to protect the woman he loved."

"What do we do now?" Jazz asked, her face turned away so that they could not see her tears.

"We bury the dead and find a way to put this right," Tristan said with determination, through gritted teeth. "If what you say is correct, if we can go back and change history, this event will never happen, yes?"

"Yes, I suppose so," Jazz replied.

"Which means Lancelot won't die here, because this timeline will not exist?"

Hope rose in Sam's mind. If they could find some other way to stop Moribund, then Tristan was correct. 'But we will know what happened. If we succeed, we will remember everything and will have to keep it secret till our dying breath. That is the curse,' she thought, 'but better that, than this.'

It took them a short while to move Lancelot in with Guinevere, and the dead into another corner of the cave. It felt like dirty work, none of them had ever touched a dead body before and the experience would change them forever. Not much had been said, it had been grisly work and something that would stick in their minds for a long time. They cleaned their hands thoroughly in the tiny river that ran through the cavern before retiring back outside the entrance. Seeing Guinevere so pale and quiet, her breath a faint whisper of movement, Sam had again felt the weight of loss. She put her hand to her mouth and had felt Jazz's arm around her side, holding her steady. She was dying, the magic in this world not strong enough to sustain her.

Sam noticed a change in Tristan, his whole demeanour had changed. A steely determination was written across his features, his every move now seemed more purposeful and assured as if the mantle of adulthood and responsibility had suddenly landed on his young shoulders, and he had embraced it in both hands willingly. 'The Squire has become a Knight without knowing it,' she thought.

"You need to tell me everything," Tristan said, when they had finished their deed. "We can stop this," he said, pointing towards the inner cavern. "If you tell me your story, there might be something that we have overlooked."

The baby Dragon had woken and Chloe had fed it with some food they had brought from Lorofax's camp. It wandered around the place like a puppy exploring its new home. At one point, it sniffed the air and trotted towards the heap of dead Skree with purpose, only for Thorfell to stop it. Even though he was only a fraction of the size, he seemed to have very quickly picked up a way of controlling the Dragon. He stood in its way and spoke to it quietly, shepherding it in a different direction while falling in beside it.

They sat near the edge of the cliff on the thin shelf, just before the drop to the ocean. Tonight, the scene was one of beauty and tranquility as if they had actually gone back to their own time. A near full moon was up and the low cloud had dissipated, leaving a line of moonlight to race across the sea towards them. The line danced and shimmered with the flow of the water. The evening was sultry, as if a precursor to a storm. Tiredness, grief and loss hung heavy in the air.

Everyone was looking out to sea, not wanting to see the tears that hid around the edges of their eyes, for fear of losing control. Lancelot was gone, Guinevere in some sort of coma and they had failed to stop Moribund from stealing the Books of Time, despite carrying out their plan perfectly. They feared they could be stuck in this time or Tristan's time, and thoughts of getting home seemed distant. The Guardians had explained their story to a wide-eyed Tristan, and he had taken it all in in his stride, believing every word, but occasionally shaking his head in disbelief of the deeds.

"How can we stop Moribund when we have no idea where he is going to be?" Sam asked.

"The man you describe. I saw that man on Avalon, he was the one who stabbed Guinevere and escaped with that box. Something came out of his arm and stabbed Guinevere. It looked almost like a tentacle that suddenly turned hard and became like a spear. It wasn't a DemonSkree, it was something else."

There was a stunned silence as the three girls and Thorfell all looked at each other. Even the baby Dragon paused in its wandering and looked towards them, as if sensing the importance of Tristan's words.

"Then we go back and stop that from happening, protect Guinevere, get the Books and save the world, boom," Chloe said enacting a exploding action with both hands. "And go home," she added.

"One problem, we are already there." Jazz pointed out.

"Oh, I hadn't thought of that," she replied looking forlorn.

"They didn't see you, they only saw me on the steps. No one else knows you were there. George saw me, he didn't see you, you were just part of the crowd."

"Then we go back and help Guinevere before she is stabbed and stop Moribund taking the Books," Chloe replied.

"We can't. If we happen to see each other, you never know what might happen! We are too close. And Guinevere can't see us either," Jazz added.

"This time travel stuff is doing my head in!" Chloe replied in frustration.

"I know where he went, Moribund, I know what route he took, we can stop him there, where no one has seen us," Tristan said.

'We must save Guinevere, though, she could die!" Sam said remembering the prone figure of Guinevere, her face ashen, her white robe covered in blood.

"She doesn't die though, she is still alive in your time, so she could not have died. If we succeed, she obviously survives to be able to meet up with you in the future!"

"But we could stop her from being stabbed," Sam said looking into the Knights eyes, which glistened in the moonlight, his eyes watering.

"How? How can you without being seen?"

"We could stop them before they reach Guinevere, it must be those three that were shuffling along in front of us on the bridge, we stop them there," she said with gusto.

"And if it is not them. They could already be in the city, just waiting for the correct time. And if it is them and we stop them on the bridge, everyone will see us," Tristan replied. Then added. "We have to stop him afterwards, in the spice market, the route he took."

"Ok, OK," Sam replied reluctantly.

"How? How are we going to stop him?" Jazz asked.

"Well, I've already thought of that," Tristan said with an all-knowing smile while getting to his feet and stepping to the cliff edge. He pointed down, then looked back to the group. "With that," he said quietly.

The three arose as one, and peered down the cliff. Lying at the bottom of the cliff, the Dragon lay dead upon the rocks. Part of the Dragon was submerged and the waves were rocking the body up and down giving it the look as if it were moving. Its head was tilted upwards, its dark eyes open as if searching the skies for help. Protruding from the snout, they glimpsed a thin shaft of wood. Moonlight cast an eerie monochromatic glow on the scene, the beams catching the glistening bands wrapped around the shaft of the wood.

"Is that what I think it is," Chloe said, excitement in her voice.

"Lancelot must have brought it with him from your time," Tristan said.

"Yes, I saw it in the cave when we arrived," Sam confirmed.

"Tristan, you are a genius," Chloe patted him on the back and nearly knocked him off the edge of the cliff.

"Wow," he said righting himself and stepping back.

"Oops, sorry."

"Try not to kill him, Chloe, we still need him," Jazz said with a faint smile.

"Why's that?" Chloe replied.

"Because who else is going to climb down there and get the spear."

"Oh, I hadn't thought of that," Tristan said mimicking Chloe's retort from earlier.

Despite the gravity of the situation, they all forced a smile and hugged each other. Jazz's eyes met Sam's. "We are going to get home, I promise," she said. Sam nodded, her lips tight, wanting to believe her friend, thinking that perhaps this time, they might just be able to get back home at last. "Yes, I want that KFC."

"McDonald's!"

"KFC!"

"What on earth are they talking about?" Tristan said, looking on quizzically.

"I've no idea," said Thorfell and the three girls smiled at the bemused duo.

CHAPTER 8 - RETURN TO AVALON

"I'll do it, I'll kill Moribund, it should be me," Tristan said.
No one replied, they hadn't thought about the fact that they were going to kill someone, even if it was Moribund and they were going to save an entire planet. The realisation dawned on them all and they looked at each other, the truth now out in the open.
"We are in this together, Tristan," Jazz said, "whether it's you who makes the killing blow, it does not matter, we are all a part of this, this is a joint responsibility, we are all in this together."
"Together, forever," Chloe said, holding out her clenched fist.
"Forever, together," Sam replied.
Jazz nodded to Tristan, who raised his fist to theirs, "Together, forever," he said a little timidly.
Jazz looked him in the eyes, "Forever together," she said with a little steel in her voice.
"Together forever, forever together," Thorfell's low voice added from on top of Chloe's left shoulder.
"It's not quite, *one for all*, is it?" Chloe said, smiling.
"It's good enough for us," Sam replied.
"Yes, yes, it is," Jazz said taking one last look towards the opening. "Rest well, I hope to see you soon, alive and well," she added quietly.
They had left the cave with heavy hearts and stood on the cliff looking down in awe as the stones retracted into the cliff face, leaving no sign of their being there. With Guinevere still alive, the magic in this world still lived on, however weak. The Dragon carcass had disappeared, swept out to sea by the rising tide or taken by some unknown predator. They had concealed the entrance as best as they could, covering it with shrubs and gorse to make it look like there was no opening at all.

Tristan carried the spear across his back, Chloe held the sleeping baby Dragon in a self-made harness across her chest, leaving her hands free. Thorfell who had grown close to the Dragon, now rested on Chloe's shoulder leaving Sam feeling a little put out. She could still feel him there, though. It was like a hat you wear for so long that when you take it off, it still feels like it is on your head. They turned their heads back towards the Thurle stone, knowing that another long day's journey lay ahead of them before they could return back to Avalon, and a final confrontation with Moribund.

"Let's do this," Chloe said, taking the lead. Tristan jogged forward to move in step with her, their eyes meeting with an embarrassed smile and simultaneous quick look away.

It wasn't until they waded back across the river, that Sam noticed that the two were now holding hands. He had gone across first and had helped Chloe out of the water. Since then, that had somehow broken the ice and they were now walking hand in hand, their fingers intertwined. 'Love has a way of showing up in the most extraordinary of places,' Sam thought, smiling. 'But why else carry on fighting for everything we know, if it isn't for the people you love? Without it, it would be pointless,' she paused in her thoughts, blinking. 'What strange and deep thoughts they were. It was almost as if someone else had put these words in her mind. Guinevere?'

"*Hello, my dear,*" the voice was faint and she knew she was the only one hearing it.

'Guinevere?'

"*It's OK, don't mourn for me, now is not the time. I need to make you aware that in your hands you hold great power that can defeat even one as strong as Moribund, remember that and remember the Bee's,*" her voice faded and stopped.

'Guinevere?' Silence answered her question. "Guinevere?" she asked out loud.

"Sam, you OK?" Jazz asked from behind her.

"Yes, sorry, I'm fine, I was just thinking of Guinevere, that's all."

They had tried to time it to reach the hole in the rock when the tide was at its lowest and they had pretty much succeeded. The rocks stretched out beyond the Thurle Stone, glistening in the morning's dim light. A small pool of water lay in front of the Stone which they recognised as the one they had come through before. The hole itself was completely out of the water, with a line of low rocks surrounding it. Crossing the beach towards the rocks, the baby Dragon who was now awake, looked up at the deserted nest and mewled once before snuggling back into Chloe, her eyes shutting again almost instantly.

"All she does is sleep," Chloe said.

"It's a baby!" Jazz exclaimed, raising her eyes, her voice edged with sarcasm. "That's what babies do!"

They had reached Lorofax's camp early in the evening, the night before, and had found more provisions and a place to sleep, safe and sound under the branches of the mighty tree. It was probably the best night's sleep they had all had for some time and they woke up stiff and aching but rejuvenated and ready to face the coming day, with renewed energy and a sense of purpose.

"This place almost feels familiar," Tristan said, "almost as if I had been here before."

The three girls looked at each other tongue tied. until Chloe retorted.

"You have, silly, we were here a few days ago."

"No, I mean, I feel like I know this place, as if I lived here," he continued.

"Probably just déjà vu," Jazz replied, her mouth dry.

'We should tell him,' Sam thought.

He shrugged his shoulders, turned away and moved on, uttering something under his breath they could not hear.

They stood before the Thurle Stone, its shadow covering the place where they stood.

"So, can you get us to come out on the bridge outside of Avalon?" Jazz asked Tristan.

"Yes," he replied with confidence.

"And we all know what the plan is. We don't know what time we will come through but it will be on that same day and probably early, so we might need to stay concealed for some time, we don't know. Everyone with the programme," she said looking from one to the other. Tristan raised his eyebrows at the word *programme*, but he got the gist of it.

They clambered around the rocks three times, then one by one, they entered the hole, with renewed hope that this was the final chapter in their quest and they would get home soon.

"Who the hell are you?" Moribund said skidding to a halt on the sandy road, both arms hugging the box, his face a scowl.

The three Guardians stood blocking his path, staffs held out in both hands, pointing towards the magician.

"We," Jazz started to say, stammering a little with nerves, "we are the ..."

She didn't have time to finish as Moribund dropped the box, lifted both hands, and black sinewy tendrils shot towards them. The tentacle like protrusions erupted from his arms, launching forth as if shot from a gun. They stretched and weaved and twisted, changing shape in the air in a kaleidoscope of shiny black flesh.

'Remember your training,' Sam thought as she saw two tendrils coming towards her. She had an instant flashback to the first time she had encountered them on the moor, when they had snatched Mr Constantine and then gone for her. She remembered the horrible icy cold slimy feel of the things around her ankles and how she had been lucky to escape. Her concentration wavered. 'Stay in the present,' she chastised herself and with incredible courage, she shut her eyes momentarily and breathed in. As planned, Chloe pulled Sam out of the way of the tendrils at the last instant, as Sam opened her eyes and exhaled deeply. Suddenly the air was full of the whirling colours of the wind. The tendrils seemed to be moving slower, and she easily ducked, pulling Jazz to the side and out of harm's way, forcing the wind to knock the protrusions off target. They glimpsed Moribund's frown of disbelief, as his tendrils missed their mark and retracted back inside him. The three

Guardians straightened, spread out and raised their shafts again.
"I don't know how you did that, but it matters not, you have signed your death warrants now," he hissed at them, spittle flying from his mouth.
'The plan was working, ' thought Sam. By now they had back-tracked along the road into a small market square. Concealed opposite the square in a small alley, Tristan stood holding the spear. Moribund was level with the alley now, a few more steps and Tristan would have a free shot at Moribund.
Moribund stopped, as if sensing his own doom.
"Come on," Jazz shouted at him.
As Moribund took one step forward and raised his arms again, Chloe's eyes left his for just the briefest of moments and peered at the shape coming out of the alley behind him. Moribund swirled in a blur of motion, that they had only seen Lancelot achieve before. He knocked the spear out of Tristan's hand while with the other, he gripped him by the neck and lifted him in the air above his head.
"No," screamed Chloe, racing forward to help Tristan.
"Chloe, no," Sam shouted and started forward. A shadowchaser appeared and jumped on the magician, followed closely by two more who almost covered the man in a seething mass of black legs and chopping mandibles. Moribund threw the choking Tristan against the nearest wall, which he crashed into and fell limply to its base, to lie prone and unmoving.
Moribund roared and his body seemed to grow, as out of his form erupted more and more dark tendrils. The shadowchasers were thrown off in all directions as his body continued to expand. In seconds, his form nearly covered the whole road, its height now level with the roof of the houses on either side. Sam's concentration had gone. A tendril shot at her, she swatted at it and missed, and then felt its icy touch constrict around her neck, choking off her air. She saw Chloe gripped around her waist and lifted off the ground while Jazz was also grabbed around the neck.
Sam felt her breath leaving her, she wheezed and the tendril constricted more. She felt her eyes bulging wide as she fought from

suffocating. 'What had Guinevere said to her, *you hold great power that can defeat even one as strong as Moribund,* what had she meant?' Instinctively she turned her staff in her hand and struck at the tendril holding her. The reaction was instantaneous. The tendril solidified for a millisecond, turned white and shattered into a thousand pieces. She fell to her knees gagging and breathing in air. 'The staff!' *'hold great power ...'* she had said. The staffs, given to them by Lancelot. They were the power that in their hands could destroy Moribund!'

"Jazz, Chloe, use the staffs, they are weapon's," she screamed over the din of falling masonry as Moribund continued to grow. No sign of the man was visible now. The form that was taking shape was that of a black Dragon, the skin looked oily and shimmered in the sunshine, as its great head started to form before their eyes.

Jazz clubbed at the tendril holding her and it shattered, throwing her to the floor. Chloe twirled her staff and struck twice in quick succession at the two tendrils holding her aloft. They shattered and she dropped to the floor to land nimbly on both feet, before turning to face Sam.

"Cool," she said nodding towards her staff.

The thing that was Moribund turned back to the Guardians shooting forth a hundred different tendrils at once. The three Guardians parried, swung and smashed their way forward, moving as one, destroying and shattering the tendrils as they moved. The Shadowchasers jumped in from the sides to block the ones that got past their defences, but they could not destroy them only block their path with their bodies. In moments they became ensnared, and a second later an oily tendril shot through Jazz's guard and wrapped itself around her staff arm. The same happened to Sam so Chloe fought on alone, swinging her staff like a lightsaber, until she too was captured, her staff hand held by two thick tendrils.

"You see," a deep bellowing voice came from the thing in front of them, "I said you had signed your death w..." The voice faltered in mid-sentence, the Dragon thing stopped moving and the air about it seemed to waver and fold in on itself. A scream, that

came from the depths of hell, erupted out of its recently formed snout, one of absolute pain. The thing screeched again and started to shrink incredibly fast, the black tendrils retracting on themselves. The three Guardians were released and they dropped to the ground alongside their shadowchasers, who immediately took a defensive position in front of them.
Moribund's form began to take form again but this time, they noticed something different. A spear, the Spear of Destiny, was protruding out of his stomach, its point covered in a dark bloodlike liquid. Moribund, his eyes wide in shock, dropped to his knees then sank forward onto his front, revealing a huge form behind him, the Knight George, one hand still holding part of the spear. It had snapped in half, but it had done its job. The Knight stared at the three Guardians, then at the shadowchasers, with interest. He raised one gloved palm.
"I believe we are on the same side," he said.
A moan from their left saw the rising form of Tristan. "Owe, ooh," he said as he rose groggily to his feet while feeling for any broken bones. A few feet in front of him sat the box with the Books of Time in it, half covered in dust and rubble. He strode forward and retrieved it, brushing it off as he approached the Knight, who stared at him with a scowl and then bemusement.
"I thought I saw you go that way," George said, pointing behind him, his face showing that he wanted to know more.
"I move fast," Tristan said with a smile.
"Not fast enough by the looks of it," George replied, having watched him clamber unceremoniously to his feet.
"Sometimes!" Tristan replied with a smile and then his expression changed to one more serious. "I believe this belongs here, get it to the Hall and guard it well."
"You sound as if you are going to run again," George replied, his deep voice smooth but challenging. "You left me up there, whatever you have been a part of here, you have to account for what you didn't do back there, you deserted me when i needed you ..." George stated.
Tristan seemed to shrink. He looked towards the group, his eyes

lingering on Chloe's for a few seconds, his face one of despair.
He strode towards them on shaky legs, then took a deep breath and straightened. "I must stay and amend for my deeds."
"No!" Chloe said loudly and he turned to face her, gripping both her hands and raising them to his lips, kissing them lightly.
"It doesn't matter where you go in time, I will find you," he said solemnly looking her in the eyes. "I promise." he added, letting her hands drop and walking to join George.
"Here, you hold this," George said smiling and passing him the box. "It will look better on you if you return with it, rather than me."
George turned back to the Guardians and raised one hand in salute.
"I don't know who you are or where you have come from, but on behalf of the people of Avalon, I thank you."
He knelt down beside the form of Moribund and turned him onto his side, peering at him closely. "He's not dead, you know," looking up at Tristan. "He is still breathing, but slowly as if in a deep sleep."
They heard the sound of footsteps on the cobbled road coming towards them down the alley. George turned his head sharply to the Guardians who had not moved.
"Go, now, unless you want to remain here," said George.
Chloe let out a sob and Jazz moved to comfort her. Behind them in the shadows of the alley Thorfell and the baby Dragon watched on, waiting.
"We have to go," Jazz said to Chloe. "We are going home," she added, smiling though tears of relief.
Sam joined them and they started off down the alley, stopping for Chloe to pick up the baby Dragon, pulling it close to her as if it were a teddy bear. Thorfell, seeing her anguish, jumped onto Sam's shoulder and they made their way towards the Bridge of Travel. As they neared it, the sound of hooves, deafeningly loud clattered down the causeway like a thousand castanets, heading back to the square.
"We are safe now, we can make our way home," said Jazz.

"Are we really going home?" Chloe questioned through her tears.
"Yes, Chloe, we are."
"I can't wait to see my mum," Sam said, with tears in her eyes.
"I've missed Rusty," Thorfell said from beside her left ear, and she laughed through her tears.
They reached the first arch and no one was about, they were alone. They walked up to the Hag Stone and all turned to look back at the magnificent sight, that was Avalon.
"Do you think we will ever see it again?" Sam asked.
"You never know, we are Guardians after all, I am sure there are lots of adventures ahead of us," Jazz replied.
"It's so beautiful," Chloe said.
"We'll be back, I'm sure," Sam said, putting an arm around the two of them, "Now let's get home, I've got a KFC waiting for me," she added with a smile.
"McDonald's!" Jazz exclaimed.
Thorfell sounded his calling, they circled the Stone three times and entered the hole, heads held high, to appear moments later in the cavern beneath the hill on Dartmoor. The Books of Time rested on the plinth untouched and unmoving.
Torches lit the walls, lighting the room just as it had been when they had left.
Putting the baby Dragon down on the stone seat, they threw themselves into each other's arms, cheering and clapping, dancing in a circle and screaming in delight, while shedding tears of joy.
A noise from the plinth and a faint light showed the Books opening. They raced to the Books and were just in time to see some writing in a strange dialect cover one page, then the Books slammed shut with a clang and the light around the edge dimmed.
"What was all that about?" Sam asked.
"No idea," Jazz replied.
"The writing was Sumerian, I think," Thorfell said standing on the plinth beside the Books. "But I have no idea, what happened there."

"Are Lancelot and Guinevere alive, do you think?" Chloe asked. By now, she had realised that she would never see Tristan again, despite his promises, and Sam could see that she was putting on a brave face.

"You know," she said putting her arm around Chloe. "that was the most romantic thing I have ever heard ... ever," she said. "And you know what, if anyone can find you and get to you, Tristan will."

"Thanks, Sam," Chloe said with a forced smile hugging her closely.

"I need to see the moor, our land," Jazz said as she started to climb the steps. The question she was asking was obvious, she wanted to find out if Lancelot and Guinevere were alive.

The sun was out, but a cold wind made them shiver a little as they made their way up onto the moor towards the Ring of Stones. It seemed almost an identical day to the one they had left on. As soon as they had appeared on the moor, they stood for a few moments breathing in the air.

"That smells so good," Sam said.

"It smells like home," Jazz replied.

They heard a faint sobbing from the ground and Thorfell was there, holding a piece of grass in his hands, tears streaming down his tiny face. "It's still here," he sobbed. Sam leant down, picked him up and put his tiny form against her cheek. "You're home, Thorfell," she said quietly.

Chloe was holding the baby Dragon in her arms and the thing was squirming and wriggling as if it was in discomfort.

"What's wrong with Peggy?" Jazz asked.

"I don't know," Chloe said worriedly. Peggy calmed as they spoke, so they decided to continue on.

They moved up the path at a steady pace, reaching the Ring of Stones in minutes. The sun was setting and night wasn't too far away. The sun looked incredibly large as it sank towards the horizon. The breeze had stopped and the evening was cool and clear. They could see for miles. Reaching a gap in the path, they stopped and peered down the gap towards a stone seat where two figures sat silently embraced as one, silhouetted by the sun.

For a moment Sam couldn't breathe, she felt a rushing inside her head, an incredible sense of relief and also one of pride. 'They'd done it,' she thought. As one, they raced down the gap towards the couple, as fast as they could.

Lancelot turned and smiled at them.

"Wo, Wo, slow down. Why the hurry?" he said, rising to meet them. Guinevere rose gracefully to her feet, her smile was one of relief. Without stopping, Sam, Jazz and Chloe literally threw themselves into their arms. Jazz and Chloe grasped Lancelot so hard, he nearly toppled backwards. Sam hugged Guinevere, tears falling freely. "Sorry," she said embarrassingly, trying to wipe them off Guinevere's top.

"Wo, Wo," Lancelot said again, "what's happened to make you act in this way, you've only been gone a few hours! What's happened?" He gripped their shoulders and gently pushed them away, staring them in the eyes for a moment. "You did it, didn't you, well done young ladies, sorry, well done Guardians." His smile couldn't have been bigger, in fact Sam thought that she had never seen him smile like that ever before.

"Well done, my dears, I knew you would do it."

"What is that?" Lancelot suddenly said, seeing the baby Dragon that Chloe had placed on the floor, with Thorfell.

"It's a baby Dragon," Chloe said smiling.

"Did you say a couple of hours?" Jazz interrupted, not believing what Lancelot had just said.

"I know I it's a baby Dragon, but what's it doing here?"

"Well, we killed its parents and it would have died if we left it there so we decided to adopt it, it's sort of an Orphan in Time now. We've called it Peggy!" She said straightening up and giving everyone one of her goofy smiles.

"Oh brother," Jazz exclaimed, raising her eyes to the sky. "You did say we have been gone for a couple of hours, didn't you?"

"Yes, yes ..." he said, his eyes never leaving Peggy's.

"I think she's very cute," Guinevere said with a wink to the girls.

"We will have to care for her here, in this realm."

"My thoughts exactly," Thorfell said.

"Oh brother," Lancelot said copying Jazz. "Thorfell, it's good to

see you, I'm sure you have much to report."
"Yes, Sire." Thorfell said bowing.
Peggy suddenly snorted, her grey snout shooting out a small plume of soot. She did it again as if was sneezing, each one louder that the last. Everyone looked on, not knowing what to do. She walked forward, let out one final snort, followed by a plume of smoke, then the folded flesh on her trunk rippled and a pair of tiny wings unfurled on either side of her body. She stood there looking back at the wings, her head held high, as if proud of her achievement. Peggy flapped them once, twice, her tail moving in sync; and then a with a few more quick flaps, to everyone's amazement she lifted off the ground, flew in a tiny circle then landed again.
"Good girl, Peggy," Chloe said.
Everyone clapped and cheered. Even Lancelot smiled and joined in, his arms tight around Guinevere's waist as they watched Peggy fly about the group before ending up in Chloe's arms, where it fell asleep in seconds.
"I think it's tired itself out," Guinevere remarked.
"Talking of sleep, you ladies need to get a decent night's sleep, we need to find Arthur tomorrow and wake him, find out where the Swords are and secure this prison once and for all."
"Oh brother!" Chloe said, dropping to the turf. "I'm going on strike!" she said and everyone laughed again.

EPILOGUE

Lancelot and Guinevere walked them back to the cavern and watched as the three Guardians disappeared through the hole, with Thorfell as their guide. Peggy mewled once then snuggled into the crook of Guinevere's arm.

"They did it," Lancelot said, his gaze still on the Hag Stone. "Formidable," he said with a strong French accent.

That day they had sat enjoying each other's company for the first time, for a very long time. They spoke, laughed and cried about the many adventures that had befallen them, and with each passing story the bonds between them grew stronger. Not once did they mention their lost children, some wounds were just too deep. Guinevere had prepared a picnic which they ate, sitting on the rocky outcrop, looking out over the moor. It wasn't long after this that the Guardians had returned with good news that their mission had been successful.

"They are incredible kids," Guinevere replied. "Will you ever tell them the truth?"

"I see no reason why!"

"Don't they deserve to know?"

"It could destroy them."

"I would like to know?"

"Of course, you would," he snapped back. Then realising his caustic remark, added "Guinevere, I meant no criticism, it's just that you see things differently from most."

She looked at him, a warm smile on her face that spoke volumes. "No offence taken, my love, now relax, I'm just bouncing questions off you that have been mulling around in my head, it's nice to have an outlet."

"It's nice to be of service, my lady," he said bowing to her, making her laugh. "Now if you will excuse me, I've an errand to run, I will be back shortly and if you like, we can talk more."

"That would be lovely," she said, reaching over and kissing him on the cheek.

Lancelot strode to the stones, walked through the circle to a pile of rocks and, retrieved a sword and dagger in a scabbard that he had concealed there; for just this sort of occasion. He wore a hooded cloak over his jeans, sweat shirt and leather walking boots. He attached the scabbard under his cloak, pulled up his hood and melted into the shadows. Thin black leather gloves kept his hands warm and fingers nimble. The moon was high and bright but a bank of clouds raced across the sky blotting out the moonlight at times.

Why could he not tell Guinevere that he had found out information that their children were alive. She definitely deserved to know, but something had held him back. He had formed the sentence in his mind and run through all the outcomes in his mind, from seeing her hearing the news with shock and possible elation or even denial. But somehow, every time he went to utter the words, his mind locked down and he couldn't get them out. He felt like a child around her at times, and he grinned thinking how he had always been putty in her hands, nothing had changed. Centuries had passed, yet here he was, still tongue tied whenever his one true love was in his presence.

He strode swiftly across the moor, his movements assured and silent in the darkness, as if he was walking in broad daylight. A coldness hung in the air and he sensed that autumn would soon turn to winter, and it wouldn't be long before snow covered these hills.

A fox appeared from a gorse bush to his left, barely five yards in front of him, then stopped abruptly seeing him. Its bushy tail swished to and fro in two quick strokes, then stopped. Their eyes locked on each other. The fox seemed to relax, as if letting out a deep breath and trotted towards Lancelot. He knelt down as the fox approached and slowly pulled his glove off and put out his hand in welcome. The fox walked up to the outstretched hand, nudged it with his jaw and then rubbed his head and torso along his arm. Lancelot reached out his other hand and gently ruffled its ear. The fox dropped onto the turf and rolled onto its side, then onto its back and back onto its side. 'It seems like you can smell and sense the real me again, my friend, I wonder if Guinevere has a factor in this?' he pondered.

He rose slowly and the fox got back to its feet, rubbed along his legs like a cat and casually walked off down the trail into the darkness. Lancelot smiled, feeling empowered that the fox had not run at first sight, he knew this was a good sign.

He reached the top of the hill and looked down into the cauldron, mostly covered in shadows from peaks and only illuminated in the centre where a clutter of bogs and thick grasses could be seen. 'I need to find out more before I speak to Guinevere, and I must therefore go into the Lion's Den to find out,' he thought. Over the centuries, he had searched above and below the Earth for any sign of their children. As a Guardian he had travelled unseen amongst the Skree, in the tunnels beneath the land on many continents and he had found nothing. Yet, one chance encounter had placed this seed of hope in his mind. Was it mind games, distraction or truth, he did not know, but tonight he planned on finding out. The young Guardians had succeeded in their quest, the next task was before them, but before they sealed the prison, he would take one more visit beneath Dartmoor to find out what he could.

He was beside the bog before he even knew it. He paused in front of one particular bog waiting for Cedric to arrive with his normal fanfare, 'He should already have appeared', he thought. Sensing something wrong, he crouched into a fighting position, while quietly drawing his sword in one hand and dagger in the other. He peered around, his luminous eyes picking out movements around him. Nothing bigger than a rabbit moved within the cauldron. 'Where was Cedric? He would never leave his post, never, the gatekeeper's position denoted that. His sole job was to offer passage to the Fairy realm, he had no other duty, no other task, so where was he? It looks like something is amiss here,' he thought and frowned beneath his hood. Never in his lifetime had a gatekeeper ever left his post, and he had lived many years on this Earth.

With his mind made up, he straightened and walked briskly to the edge, braced himself and sprang out into the bog, disappearing in an instant beneath the surface with the faintest of plops. He landed on both feet and sprang forward, his momentum taking him forward a few steps until he found his balance. He stopped again, controlling his breathing, listening. Not a sound could be heard, the place felt like a tomb. He waited a few seconds more for his eyes to acclimatise to the darkness, then looked around him, only his head moving from side to side. It looked as it did before. Everything looked deserted and covered in layers of dust. He turned looking behind him and was met with a similar sight. He could sense that no one was near so he relaxed, straightened and looked down at the floor. The dust upon the floor had been disturbed by many feet, all non-human, all leading away from him. Something in the centre of the disturbance had been dragged along and he wondered if this had been Cedric. 'Had he been captured? Surely, they would not be brazen enough to kidnap a gatekeeper? Or even kill a gatekeeper?' The disturbance seemed recent, the dust had hardly settled.

He followed the trail easily, his eyes gleaming in the dark, picking out the marks. He reached the end of the hall and spotted a hole that had been smashed through the back wall. Then, looking at the rubble, he realised that it had been made from the other side, where solid rock stretched to the ceiling. Something had burst through here. So, this is where the Erlking came from, with his Skree in tow. The footprints continued on and through the opening. He had plans on making a different way into the Skree underworld, but this opening seemed too good to leave; and if Cedric had been captured, he might be able to free him. A distant sound came from the opening and he turned his ear towards the darkness. A faint roaring could be heard far off, a sound that sent a sliver of fear though his normally calm mind. He entered the opening crouching low, sword held out. A round hastily dug tunnel had been dug out of the rock leading into the depths, held up in places by rocks or wood. He kept to one side, moving fast, making no sound. He reached an opening and paused again, sensing movement ahead. A small circular cavern lay before him with six exits leading off, all recently dug, bar one. He pressed himself against the wall behind a beam of wood, his form becoming just another shadow, as seven DemonSkree entered in a hurry from one tunnel and exited in the opposite hole. They passed barely a yard away from him but none of them sensed his presence. The DemonSkree were so large that they had to crouch low and move in single file along the small tunnels. The roaring was louder now and coming from the tunnel to the right of where the DemonSkree had entered. Peering around the cavern, he checked for movement then hurried across and into right hand tunnel. He saw two figures coming toward him so he ducked into a small alcove, making himself as small as he could, becoming one with the shadows. Two Skree shuffled along and passed him, one brushing its scaly arm across Lancelots cloak, but it did not stop. The Skree disappeared into the cavern, Lancelot moved on, the tunnel leading upwards now. Ahead of him a faint glow emanated from the end of the tunnel and the sound was becoming almost deafening. It was like a wave of noise, a roar of a thousand inhuman voices followed by a huge cracking, then banging noise as a thousand things hit the stone all at once. And then silence for the briefest of moments before it started again. He reached an opening and realised he had come out high up on a cliff. A few boulders littered the edge and he crouched behind them, looking down on a scene that made his blood turn to ice.

He had never seen this cavern before, it was huge, one of the biggest underground caves he had ever seen. He was about sixty feet up from the ground, on a ledge that ran the entire length of the cave. The roof was another twenty feet above him and enshrouded in darkness. Great columns of rock were interspersed within the cavern at regular intervals, supports put there in a bygone era. Torches, in their hundreds, littered the walls and stood in iron braziers, picking out the inhuman things that lay within.

"Sacré bleu," he whispered to himself, a cold sweat forming on his troubled brow.

Below him stood a seething mass of Skree, Erlking and more DemonSkree than he had ever seen since the great battles of yesteryear. He tried counting by columns and got to an approximate figure of a couple of thousand at least. 'They were planning for war all along, they would annihilate us with this force.' he thought to himself. The whole mass had their backs to him and were facing some sort of natural stage area. The inhuman sound was coming from the roaring of the creatures followed by the synchronised stamping of their feet, and the banging down on the rock of all the different weapons they held in their hands. 'They were dressed for war,' his mind racing, 'we are too late,' he thought in panic.

On the stage the instantly recognisable form of Moribund stood facing his army. The noise had stopped and he started to speak, the whole cavern going quiet as his voice echoed around the cavern.

"My friends," he started, stretching his arms wide, "the time of our victory over the Humans is nearly upon us," he paused for effect and a great roar went up. "Armies from all over the world are awaiting my order, my word, to take control of this planet, to make the Earth ours, once and for all. Our task is simple, we retrieve the *Books of Time* and nothing can stop us. Once they are within my possession, then we cannot be stopped, the Earth will be ours, we will be free," he shouted the last words out and another roar of approval went up.

"However," he said holding his hand up for the crowd to stop. "We have a Guardian to deal with, one who will not let the Books go lightly, so I have a secret weapon, actually two secret weapons that will win us the day." The army roared again, enrapt with every word he spoke. He beckoned behind him to two dark openings in the rock and as one, a form emerged from both. A loud roaring erupted as soon as the figures came into the light, and kept going until they stopped beside Moribund. He turned and smiled at one, and then the other, before putting one arm around each.

Lancelot's mind exploded, his thoughts so confused that he could not form any words, yet a part of him knew he couldn't form any words which made it worse.

The two figures were Human, one a man and one a woman. They seemed to be young, but it was difficult to judge from Lancelot's distance. The man was huge, well over six and a half foot. He dwarfed Moribund who had difficulty reaching his arm up to wrap around the man's shoulder. The man's face looked passive, almost unfocussed as if he was in a dream, or drugged. A massive two-handed broadsword rested across his shoulder. His physique was huge, he was all muscle and sinew. He wore long leather boots and shorts, with a sort of loose-fitting top that hung tight in places upon his large torso. But it was his features that had made Lancelot's mind go numb. The man had long flowing black hair, and even from this distance, he could see the green tint of his eyes that were so like Guinevere's. His high forehead, long Roman nose and strong mouth sat upon a face he had seen a million times over in a mirror, his own.

"Sacré bleu, that is my son," he said as he peered across at the woman knowing what he was going to see even before his eyes focussed on her. She stood at least six feet tall, lithe and slim of build. She also wore long boots, with a short leather dress that showed strong muscular legs. Her torso and arms were wrapped in a fine chain mail armour that looked like interwoven fish scales. The flickering torch light glinted off it every time she move, casting dazzling beams of light around the cavern. Her long blonde hair was tied in a ball behind her head and her eyes were an even lighter shade of green. Her pretty face was dirty and unkempt, yet she looked so like Guinevere, he almost believed it was her. She carried a bow and he glimpsed a notch of arrows on her back.

"They were alive," he said to himself. He had seen enough, he had to get back to Guinevere, to the Council. They must believe him this time. Otherwise it would be too late. And then he would form a plan to free his children, to bring them home.

Shaking a little, he glided down the tunnel, his senses reeling, his concentration and focus gone. He stumbled around a bend and ran straight into a Skree, bowling them both over. Immediately his focus crystallised, his training kicked in and he kicked out pushing the Skree away, giving himself room to bring up his sword and ...

"You," the thing grunted getting to its feet. The Skree standing in front of him in the cavern had a dirty cloth bandage wrapped around one leg.

"You," Lancelot said, recognising the Skree he had helped to return to the prison.

"I don't want to kill you," Lancelot said holding his sword out, pointing it at the creature.

"And I don't want to die," it replied in its deep guttural voice.

"Then let me pass and I will be gone and no one will be the wiser."

"Apart from me. Not all of us want to fight, you know," it said.

Another roar went up behind them and more stamping of feet and clanging of weapons.

"I beg to differ," he replied, pointing his dagger towards the sound.

"Not all of us want to fight," it repeated.

"That's an army in there and somehow it's found a way to get out and when it does, war will be its calling," he said through gritted teeth. "I also want to stop this war now," he heard himself say.

"I know who they are going to use to break free. If I get him for you, it will give you time to try and stop this, will you try to stop this?" the Skree asked, then added, "We have families who are tired of this, we are happy here, this is our home."

The Skree was speaking the truth, Lancelot could see this. His mind was reeling again with this news. 'Who? Cedric, of course, they could use his special talents to open the prison long enough for this army to come out. One night would be all it takes and the Books would be Moribund's, and history would be rewritten. Why had I not thought of this?'

"If you agree to try, I will get your gatekeeper, it will stall the process long enough, I hope, to make the difference," it paused again, "Call it a token of peace, from my race to yours."

Lancelot lowered his weapon. "OK, thank you."

"Then go, meet me in the Elfin chamber, wait for us there, I will bring your gatekeeper."

Without another word or looking back, the Skree disappeared into one of the tunnels leaving Lancelot free to make his way back towards the surface. Later he was standing in the shadows of the overhang, his mind still going around in circles when he heard the faint sound of someone approaching. Cedric appeared first stumbling over the pile of rubble, his arms tied, followed closely by the Skree.

"Cedric," Lancelot said quietly, pleased to see his old friend.

"Lancelot," he replied gruffly.

'He was embarrassed that he had been captured and had left his post,' Lancelot thought with a faint smile. The Skree cut his arms loose with one of its talons and Cedric joined Lancelot. The Skree stood half in, half out of the opening, looking back worriedly every now and then.

"Thank you," Lancelot said sincerely. "Are you going to be OK?" he asked thinking how much the Skree had put his own life at risk.

"No one has seen me, I can blend in, they will not know who set him free or if he just freed himself. Almost everyone was in the big cavern," it said.

"Then, I thank you again, friend."

"They call me Krall," it said.

"Then, I thank you, Krall," Lancelot said and bowed. Krall turned to go and then stopped.

"You know," he hissed slightly, "we were brothers once, a long time ago."

"Brothers?"

"Our races worked together, many thousands of years ago."

"What!" A niggling thought began to work away in the back of Lancelot's head, some distant memory.

"For our masters, the true rulers."

"Masters? True rulers? What are you talking about? Who are you? How do you know so much?" Lancelot was looking around him, feeling that time was running out, he had to get out quickly. The Skree was also looking agitated, forever glancing back as if he should not be lingering either.

"The Anunaki. I cannot stay, I must go, before I am caught. I will

meet with you by the Black Stone in two nights time. I will explain then. Will you be there? Can you open the way?"
"Yes, yes," Lancelot replied, his breath coming fast. "Thank you," he added hastily and bowed. When he rose up and looked, Krall was gone.
They moved quickly to the other end of the chamber, through the doors, along another chamber lined with alcoves to reach the huge double doors. Lancelot retrieved a key from his cloak, put it into the keyhole, pushed the door open and then they were back onto the moor again, the crisp coldness of the night refreshing and calming all in one. Cedric shut the door quietly and the whole thing merged into the rock face disappearing from sight in the darkness.
"Thank you," he said to Lancelot.
I didn't come for you,' he was about to say, then thought better of it. "My pleasure," he said with a grin, "Just like the old times," he added, slapping the gatekeeper on the back in fun." I was always having to save your sorry a..."
"Now look here, Lancelot," he started to reply in annoyance before seeing the man's eyes twinkle.
He snorted once, then twice and Lancelot laughed aloud. "You know, Cedric, I haven't heard your laugh for ages, it's good to hear. Now come, I need you with me to talk to Guinevere and the Council, I need you by my side as proof."
"But I am the gatekeeper," Cedric said proudly as if nothing else mattered.
"Not today you're not," Lancelot said. "Come on, we don't have a second to spare. We've got a war to stop!"

Printed in Poland
by Amazon Fulfillment
Poland Sp. z o.o., Wrocław